SO-AIJ-658

JUST WHO *WAS* SHE, ANYWAY?

Melanie started up the stairs, dragging her sleeping bag behind her. Suddenly she stopped midway up and looked around.

"This is Christie's house," she muttered under her breath. "And the father I just said good morning to was Christie's father. He acted as if I was Christie. Why didn't he notice that I'm Melanie?"

She looked down at her legs. They were too long. And the powder-blue sweat suit she was wearing was the one Christie had been wearing the night before.

Melanie swallowed hard, trying to fight down the wad of panic that was gathering in her throat. Leaving the sleeping bag on the stairs, she raced to Christie's room and looked in the dresser mirror. The face that looked back at her belonged to Christie Winchell.

"Oh, my gosh!" she gasped. Then she pulled a strand of hair out in front of her face and looked at it. It was blond instead of the reddish-brown that it should be.

Looking back into the mirror she studied the face. It was Christie's face, and she was in Christie's body.

"But that can't be," she whispered in astonishment. "I'm Melanie. Melanie Edwards."

Or was she?

Bantam Skylark Books by Betsy Haynes
Ask your bookseller for the books you have missed

THE AGAINST TAFFY SINCLAIR CLUB
TAFFY SINCLAIR STRIKES AGAIN
TAFFY SINCLAIR, QUEEN OF THE SOAPS
TAFFY SINCLAIR AND THE ROMANCE MACHINE
  DISASTER
BLACKMAILED BY TAFFY SINCLAIR
TAFFY SINCLAIR, BABY ASHLEY, AND ME
TAFFY SINCLAIR AND THE SECRET ADMIRER
  EPIDEMIC
TAFFY SINCLAIR AND THE MELANIE MAKE-OVER
THE TRUTH ABOUT TAFFY SINCLAIR
THE GREAT MOM SWAP
THE GREAT BOYFRIEND TRAP

Books in The Fabulous Five Series

1 SEVENTH-GRADE RUMORS
2 THE TROUBLE WITH FLIRTING
3 THE POPULARITY TRAP
4 HER HONOR, KATIE SHANNON
5 THE BRAGGING WAR
6 THE PARENT GAME
7 THE KISSING DISASTER
8 THE RUNAWAY CRISIS
9 THE BOYFRIEND DILEMMA
#10 PLAYING THE PART
#11 HIT AND RUN
#12 KATIE'S DATING TIPS
#13 THE CHRISTMAS COUNTDOWN
#14 SEVENTH-GRADE MENACE
#15 MELANIE'S IDENTITY CRISIS
#16 THE HOT-LINE EMERGENCY
#17 TEEN TAXI
#18 CELEBRITY AUCTION
#19 THE BOYS-ONLY CLUB

THE FABULOUS FIVE

The Fabulous Five in Trouble

BETSY HAYNES

A BANTAM SKYLARK BOOK®
NEW YORK · TORONTO · LONDON · SYDNEY · AUCKLAND

RL 5, 009–012

THE FABULOUS FIVE
IN TROUBLE
A Bantam Skylark Book / August 1990

*Skylark Books is a registered trademark of Bantam Books, a division of
Bantam Doubleday Dell Publishing Group, Inc. Registered in U.S. Patent
and Trademark Office and elsewhere.*

*All rights reserved.
Copyright © 1990 by Betsy Haynes and James Haynes.
Cover art copyright © 1990 by Andrew Bacha.
No part of this book may be reproduced or transmitted in any form or by
any means, electronic or mechanical, including photocopying, recording, or
by any information storage and retrieval system, without permission in
writing from the publisher.
For information address: Bantam Books.*

ISBN 0-553-15814-7

Published simultaneously in the United States and Canada

*Bantam Books are published by Bantam Books, a division of Bantam Double-
day Dell Publishing Group, Inc. Its trademark, consisting of the words
"Bantam Books" and the portrayal of a rooster, is Registered in U.S. Patent
and Trademark Office and in other countries. Marca Registrada. Bantam
Books, 666 Fifth Avenue, New York, New York 10103.*

PRINTED IN THE UNITED STATES OF AMERICA

CWO   0 9 8 7 6 5 4 3 2 1

CHAPTER

1

"Is it true that The Fabulous Five is breaking up?"

Jana Morgan slammed her locker door and whirled around to face Alexis Duvall, who had just spoken.

"Where did you hear a thing like that?" Jana demanded.

"A lot of places," said Alexis, shrugging. "Everybody's talking about it. Is it true?"

"No!" said Jana emphatically. "And I wish people would stop spreading *rumors* about us."

Alexis backed away. "Oh . . . sorry, Jana. I was just repeating what I heard."

"Well, there's nothing wrong between The Fabu-

1

lous Five, and you can tell everybody that," Jana snapped.

"If you say so," Alexis said with disbelief in her voice.

"I do say so," answered Jana. "And Christie, Katie, Beth, and Melanie say so, too." Glowering, she turned on her heel and headed toward the yearbook office.

In spite of what she had just said to Alexis, Jana knew the truth was, there was trouble right between her and her friends, Beth Barry, Christie Winchell, Katie Shannon, and Melanie Edwards. The five of them had been best friends since they'd first met back in Mark Twain Elementary school, but for the past few weeks it had seemed to Jana that they were drifting apart. They were each spending more and more time with other people, and whenever they were together, all they did was argue. Jana couldn't figure out what to do about it. She sighed and pushed open the door to *The Wigwam* office. Funny Hawthorne, the seventh-grade coeditor of the yearbook, was hard at work at their table with glossy photographs spread all around her.

"Hi," said Funny, her wide blue eyes sparkling. Funny was a member of The Fantastic Foursome, a rival clique that sometimes clashed with The Fabulous Five. Even though the two groups didn't get along, Jana and Funny were becoming close friends. They had been staying after school almost every day to work on the yearbook.

"Hi, Funny," answered Jana, putting her things down on the corner of the worktable and gazing around at the stacks of photographs. "We still have a lot of work to do, don't we?"

"Yup," Funny mumbled. "The deadline for the seventh-grade section is coming up."

Jana picked up one of the piles of pictures and thumbed through them. The faces of her classmates at Wakeman Junior High stared back at her. There were pictures of the members of the academic Super Quiz team, the judges on the Teen Court, and shots of the homework hot-line center, the class officers' meetings, the cheerleaders, the sports teams, the school plays, and even several pictures of herself and her boyfriend, Randy Kirwan, being crowned seventh-grade Mr. and Miss Wakeman Junior High. It usually made Jana feel proud to see at least one member of The Fabulous Five in almost every picture. Christie was on both the Super Quiz and homework hot-line teams. Katie was a judge on the Teen Court. Beth and Melanie were cheerleaders, and Beth was in all the school plays and on lots of committees. They were certainly great friends, except that lately . . .

Jana shook away the troubling thoughts that were beginning to gather in her mind and sat down to arrange pictures of the cheerleaders. Once she had finished laying them out in an interesting way, she would write captions for them and show them to their faculty advisor, Mr. Neal, for his approval.

Jana stopped a moment and dug a tissue out of her purse and blew her nose.

"Got a cold?" asked Funny.

"Yeah," answered Jana. "And it seems to be getting worse." Funny gave Jana a sympathetic look. "I promise I won't give it to you," said Jana.

"That's okay," responded Funny, smiling. She hesitated, then added, "Jana, can I tell you something?"

Jana looked up. "Sure."

"Tammy Lucero lives on the same street as Shawnie Pendergast," Funny went on, "and she said Tony Calcaterra has been over at Shawnie's house several times in the last couple of weeks. I thought since he's Katie's boyfriend, I ought to tell you."

The news astounded Jana. Tony and Shawnie had liked each other last year when they both went to Copper Beach Elementary, but Tony was going out with Katie now. Katie would be crushed if the rumor was true. "I know Tammy's part of The Fantastic Foursome," said Jana, "but she gossips a lot. I don't think Tony would do a thing like that."

Funny shrugged. "I know Tammy's a gossip, but I believed her. She said Tony's bike was out in front of Shawnie's all afternoon on Saturday, and she's seen him coming and going a few times in the evening. I really don't think she's making it up," she said almost apologetically. "I thought you might want to say something to Katie."

"Maybe," said Jana. "But I would like more than Tammy's word on it."

"*Achoo!*" Jana grabbed for her purse and dug out another tissue. "*Achoo!*" She managed to cover her nose just in time.

"Gee, you've really got a bad cold," said Funny. "Why don't you go home? I'll finish these layouts. You don't want to get sick and miss the dance."

Jana blew her nose, which was getting red and tender from so much blowing. "Or have a big red nose, which wouldn't go at all with the dress Mom and I laid away at Tanninger's. You don't really mind if I leave?" she asked.

"Naw. Actually I'm being selfish." Funny laughed. "It's better for you to rest and get over your cold than get really sick and be out for a week. I think I'd actually commit suicide if that happened." She collapsed against the back of her chair, pretending to be dead. Then she giggled and opened one eye to peek at Jana.

"Thanks," said Jana, giving Funny a look of appreciation. Leave it to her to understand, she thought. Funny's a terrific friend. Jana slipped on her jacket, picked up her purse, and waved good-bye to Funny with her fingers.

Jana decided to take the long way home. If she went the usual way, she would have to pass Bumpers, the fast-food restaurant where the kids from Wakeman hung out. The rest of The Fabulous Five was sure to be inside, and Jana knew they would pressure her to join them. Not only that, one of them would probably say something about all the time she was spending with Funny. But as she detoured a couple of blocks and cut down Shawnie Pendergast's street, she saw something that made her wish she had gone past Bumpers instead. Parked in front of Shawnie's house, as big as life, was Tony Calcaterra's bicycle.

Earlier that afternoon Melanie Edwards had glanced around the classroom as her history teacher, Mr. Naset, handed out the test papers. Shane Arrington was looking in her direction and he flashed her a big smile. She smiled back, putting all the personality she could into it. Maybe Shane would ask her to the school dance, she thought. Or if not, Scott Daly surely would. She liked them both a lot and couldn't bear to think of either one's going to the dance with someone else.

Just then she felt someone looking at her from the other side of the room. Turning quickly, she came eye to eye with Katie Shannon, three rows over. Katie had a disgusted look on her face, and she might as well have been wearing a neon sign that said MELANIE EDWARDS IS BOY CRAZY!

Melanie slumped back in her seat. Why can't Katie just get off my case? she wondered. Being a judge on Teen Court has turned her into a regular busybody. It's none of her business if I flirt with Shane in history class.

Ignoring Katie, Melanie stole another glance at Shane, who by now had turned his attention to his history test. "Thanks a lot, Katie," she whispered under her breath.

"Har-umph!"

Melanie was jerked back to reality by Mr. Naset, who was standing over her waiting to give her a test paper.

"All right, class. You've got nearly, let's see . . . fifty minutes to finish," said Mr. Naset. "I'd advise you to take your time doing it. Since it represents forty percent of the semester grade, it's obviously a very important test for you. Good luck."

Melanie gave a little moan as she thumbed through the pages of the test. It looked hard. Why did exams have to be given just before the school dance? Didn't the teachers know that everyone was too excited to think about tests? The dance was all anyone could talk about, except for Katie, of course. Melanie let out a huge sigh, wishing that Katie weren't so serious all the time. Then she flipped back to the first page, picked up her pencil, and started reading the first question.

"Look at those idiots," exclaimed Katie Shannon. "They're acting like a bunch of first-graders."

It was after school and Katie was sitting with Melanie, Beth, and Christie in a booth at Bumpers. They were watching Richie Corrierro, Matt Zeboski, and Clarence Marshall pushing and shoving each other in front of the old Wurlitzer jukebox as they tried to put money in and select songs. Mr. Matson, the owner of Bumpers, was frowning at them from behind the cash register. Katie was sure that Mr. Matson couldn't believe how childishly the boys were behaving either. She was glad Tony Calcaterra wasn't there and acting up like the others.

"It's getting near exam time," said Beth. "It's making the guys crazy."

"Not just the guys," said Melanie, rolling her eyes. "I feel as if I've got to break out of this penitentiary. We had a humongous test in history today and it counted for forty percent of our grade."

"Tell me about it," said Christie, bowing her head and rubbing her temples. "You ought to try taking an honors class in history. I've been studying every night until midnight." The red veins in her eyes told Katie that she wasn't exaggerating.

"You try too hard," observed Beth. "Did you ever think of making a B?"

Christie looked up at her but didn't respond.

"You think you've got it bad," said Katie, annoyed that a brain like Christie had the nerve to complain about homework. "Teen Court has more cases right now than it's had all year. Every time we get a new list I'm afraid Tony's name is going to be on it."

"That's what you get for dating a habitual criminal," Melanie said sarcastically, and Katie wasn't sure whether or not she was teasing.

"It must be tough making the right decisions in all those cases," Beth said quickly. "I don't know how in the world you do it."

Katie threw Beth a grateful look. At least Beth was trying to keep peace in the group. "It really isn't all that hard," Katie admitted. "We all know what right and wrong is. You just have to find out if the person actually did what he or she is accused of. Usually it's pretty clear, or they wouldn't be before the court in the first place."

"But aren't there times when you aren't so sure?" Beth asked.

"Hardly ever," responded Katie emphatically. "You just keep burrowing in until you find out the truth."

"Our hangin' judge," muttered Christie.

"That's not fair," said Katie, feeling angry again. "Someone has to remind people what the rules are. If we didn't, they'd keep bending them until there weren't any rules at all." She looked around the table waiting for someone to challenge her.

"Sorry," said Christie.

Beth changed the subject. "Where's Jana, anyway?"

"I saw her at her locker," said Melanie. "She was working on *The Wigwam* after school today. She sounded awful. She has a cold, and I think she's been trying to do too much."

"She ought to try being on *all* the dance committees, the way I am," said Beth. "Then she'd know what busy is. Does everyone have their dates all set for the dance?"

Christie ignored her question. "We're all busy," she snapped. "Jana's got the yearbook, Katie's got Teen Court, I've got the homework hot line, and Mel's on the refreshments committee for the dance."

Beth arched an eyebrow and looked at Christie with an air of superiority. "Well, I'm on the decorations committee, the entertainment committee, *and* the refreshments committee for the dance. So there!"

"Whoop-de-do," said Katie derisively. "They were all your decisions." Beth stuck out her lower lip and frowned at Katie.

Katie held her tongue and looked away. Taffy Sinclair was sitting in a nearby booth with Cory Dillon, looking at them with a curious expression. She was probably dying to know what was going on. Taffy had been their archenemy back in Mark Twain Elementary school and she would be delighted if she knew how much trouble The Fabulous Five had been having lately.

What was wrong with everyone, anyway? Katie wondered as she glanced back at her friends. They were really picking on each other. Christie thought she had it tough because she was on the homework hot-line team and had to make all A's to keep her parents happy, Beth thought everybody should be impressed because she was on all of the dance committees, and Melanie was fretting over one measly little history test. Big deal, she thought. None of them really had to make the kind of important decisions she did on the Teen Court. Being fair *wasn't* easy when you had to decide on punishments for kids you knew. But someone had to do it, and she was proud of what she and the other judges were doing. She decided not to talk about Teen Court again. Her friends just didn't understand.

Christie Winchell walked into the homework hot-line center that evening carrying an armload of books. Tim Riggs was leaning back with his feet up on the desk in his cubicle and waved hello. Pam Wolthoff and Mr. Snider, the team sponsor, were discussing something at Mr. Snider's table at the back of the room.

Christie gave a big sigh as she plopped her books on her desk and took off her jacket. She hoped there weren't many calls from kids this evening. The pile of her own homework made Mount Everest look like an anthill. Why did teachers always have to give tests on the same day so that you couldn't spread out the studying? The honors history class was especially hard. Miss Jamal was a stickler about students' remembering dates for all the nitty-gritty little events that no one in her right mind cared about anyway.

While everyone else was talking about the end of school and the big dance, she had more serious things on her mind. If she wanted to get a scholarship to one of the better colleges in the country, she had to concentrate on keeping her grades up. Jon Smith had seemed hurt at first when she turned down his invitation to the dance, but she had told him more than once she didn't want to date him steadily, and he had been asking her for dates a lot lately. The more she thought about it, there wasn't any other boy she wanted to go with either.

Christie methodically arranged her books in the order that she had to study them, sharpened her pencils, got out a new pad of paper, and took the first book off the stack. Naturally the telephone rang just at that moment.

Christie flipped her pencil in the air disgustedly and reached for the phone. "Homework hot-line center. How may I help you?"

The caller had questions about algebra, and Christie had a hard time getting him to understand how to work the problems. "Look," she said firmly. "If you'll just go back and *read* the previous chapter, you'll understand how to do it."

"Well, *excuse me!*" the caller exclaimed. "You don't

have to bite my head off. I thought you were supposed to help people, not yell at them."

Christie took a deep breath. He was right. She had no business talking to him that way. What was happening to her patience? She was flying off the handle a lot lately. She rubbed her forehead and said, "I'm sorry. Let's start all over. If you take the first formula and add it to the second . . ."

By the end of the evening, Christie was exhausted. It seemed as if she had answered at least twenty or thirty phone calls, and they had all been harder than usual. On top of that, she hadn't been able to do any studying of her own, and that meant another late night for her.

And Beth has the nerve to tell me that *she's* trying too hard, thought Christie. All Beth was doing was having a good time being on dance committees. That was nothing but socializing. If she put in as much time on things that counted, such as her studies, she might have a reason to criticize me, Christie decided, and raised her chin defiantly. But not until then!

Beth Barry hung up the phone. Let's see, she thought, picking up her pad of paper and pencil. Mandy McDermott had just agreed to head the committee to buy paper cups and napkins and stuff. Beth put a check by Mandy's name. Whitney Larkin will keep track of the ticket sales, and Shane Arrington will be master of ceremonies. I've got someone in charge of everything, she thought. Beth smiled to herself. It was fun being on committees and talking to people who paid attention to her. It's not like at home, where I have to yell my head off to get my own family to notice me. And it's sure not like being with The Fabulous Five, where no one does anything but pick on each other anymore.

CHAPTER

2

*W*hen Jana got home, her mother called out from the kitchen, "Hi, sweetheart. You're early."

"I didn't do much work on the yearbook. I've got an algebra and a social studies test tomorrow and I have to study," answered Jana. "Besides that, this cold is really bugging me. But what are *you* doing home so early?"

"I had a dentist appointment, so I took the whole afternoon off," her mother replied. "I've been puttering in the kitchen ever since I got home."

Jana brightened. "What's for dinner?" she asked.

"Your nose must be really stuffed up if you have to ask," said her mother, laughing. "Lasagna, salad, and garlic bread. I thought you'd approve. It's Pink's favorite, too," she added almost apologetically. She stopped and looked closely at Jana. "You really don't look as if you feel well."

Jana stood still as her mother put a hand on her forehead to check her temperature. Her mother and natural father had divorced when Jana was small, and her mother had recently married Wallace Pinkerton, whom everyone called Pink. He worked at the same newspaper where Jana's mother was classified ads manager.

"At least you don't feel hot," said Mrs. Pinkerton. "Just don't get overtired, okay? Remember what happened to Melanie when she tried to do too much."

Jana grimaced. Earlier in the year Melanie had gotten overly tired and contracted mononucleosis. Kids at school had teased her about having the "kissing disease" until The Fabulous Five banded together to set the record straight. Jana sighed. That was in the good old days. She seriously doubted that The Fabulous Five would band together like that anymore.

Jana dropped her books on the desk in her room and went to the bathroom to wash up. As usual the tiny bathroom in their apartment was overcrowded. Her mother's panty hose hung from the shower-curtain rod, and Pink's dirty socks were lying behind the door where he had forgotten them. Besides her mother's and her things, Pink's electric razor, after-shave lotion, deodorant, and hair spray were on the counter, and she could hardly find the soap.

Jana sighed. She liked Pink a lot, but things had been this way ever since he had moved in with them, and she felt almost squeezed out of her own apartment. Even the living room was crowded with his bowling trophies.

As she washed her face, she looked again at Pink's things on the counter. She needed to come up with an idea for a Father's Day gift for him and one for her father in Poughkeepsie. She hadn't saved much money though. It would be tough to buy both of them something worthwhile with her small allowance.

Thinking about Father's Day always made Jana feel sad. It reminded her of the summer before the sixth grade when her father had written her and said he would take her on a two-week vacation out west. She had gotten all excited and had waited anxiously for him to come for her, but he never did. After that her mother had told Jana that he was an alcoholic and couldn't help doing things like that. Deep down Jana still felt that if he only loved her enough, he still might have come or would at least write her once in a while.

She inspected herself closely in the mirror. "What's wrong with me?" she whispered. Suddenly she desperately wanted to talk to someone. Someone who could help her sort out her confused feelings.

She had always been able to talk to Beth at moments like this. Beth had been her very best friend for as long as she could remember.

Jana started for the phone and then stopped, letting her arms drop to her sides. It was no use calling Beth. She was always too busy for her best friends lately. Besides, Jana wasn't so sure that Beth would understand anymore.

Melanie scuffed along on her way to school the next morning. She preferred taking a chance on being late to having to stand at The Fabulous Five's favorite spot by the fence and listen to everyone gripe at each other. It was depressing to hear Jana complaining about her home life all the time, Beth talking about all the activities she was in, Christie crabbing about all the pressure she was under, and Katie getting on her case about being gullible and boy crazy. It would be great to get away from all the nagging that was going on.

Dekeisha Adams and Marcie Bee were fun. Maybe she would eat lunch with them today. Melanie shook her head. That might make the other members of The Fabulous Five angry, and she didn't want that to happen. She just wanted them to be friends again, the way they used to be.

"Hey, Melanie! Wait up!"

Melanie turned as Mona Vaughn came running up behind her.

"Hi, Mona," said Melanie. "Where have you been? I haven't seen you around lately."

"Oh, I just decided to take a few days off and watch my favorite soaps," Mona answered between pants. When she saw Melanie's eyes open in surprise, she giggled. "Only kidding. I had the flu."

"There's a lot of that going around," said Melanie. "But with exams, it's a tough time to be absent. Did someone tell you what the assignments were in your classes?"

Mona shrugged. "I think that I got most of them. I still have some reading in English and history to do, but I'll catch up."

Melanie turned to look at Mona. "You did know we had a test in history while you were absent, didn't you?"

Mona gave her a blank look. "Gosh, no." Then her expression changed to apprehension. "Wow, Mel. What will I do? I haven't studied, and you know that Mr. Naset always makes us take the tests we miss on the day we come back to class."

"That's right," said Melanie. "Which means that you only have until this afternoon to study for it. Eeek! What *are* you going to do?"

By now Mona looked totally dismal. "Gosh. I don't know. I'm not doing very well in history. I can't afford to flunk another test."

"*Another* test?" Melanie asked in surprise.

Mona nodded. "Like I said, I'm not doing very well in history."

"Oh, Mona. You've just got to do well in this one, or you'll fail the course. I hate to tell you, but it counts *forty percent* of the total grade."

Mona was silent as they walked toward the school. Melanie felt sorry for her. Mona had never had a lot going for her to begin with. In elementary school she had followed Taffy Sinclair around like a puppy. Everyone always thought that it was because Mona was so homely and Taffy so beautiful that Mona hoped some of Taffy's good looks would rub off on her. Things were going better for Mona now at Wacko. With the help of The Fabulous Five she had learned to fix her hair and bring out her best features so that she wasn't homely anymore. She even had Matt Zeboski for a boyfriend now. But even with that, Mona still had her problems, and now this. Melanie had never felt so much sympathy for her.

"Maybe we could get together at lunch and review the chapters," Melanie offered.

The smile she expected from Mona didn't materialize. Instead, Mona kicked a rock into the grass and said, "What good would that do? I haven't even read the chapters."

Melanie sighed, but then Mona blinked as if a great idea had just occurred to her. "Hey, I've got it, Mel. Why don't you write down all the test answers that you can remember, and I'll memorize them? That way, at least I'll pass. Would you do it?"

"What?" Melanie asked in amazement. "That would be cheating."

Mona looked at the ground, coloring slightly, but when she turned to Melanie again, her face was intense and her eyes were pleading. "I *know* it sounds bad," she admitted. "But what else can I do? I didn't know that there was a test. And it's just for this one time. I'll never ask again. I promise. Besides, you're my friend. If I can't ask you for help, who can I ask?"

Melanie's mind was reeling. *Why don't you ask someone else?* she wanted to shout. *Ask Matt.* But Matt wasn't in their class. *Ask . . . Ask . . .* Surely there was someone else Mona could ask, but Melanie knew that Mona didn't have many friends, especially friends who were taking Mr. Naset's history. Melanie had a sinking feeling that she was trapped.

Swallowing hard, she turned toward Mona, who stood beside her looking even more pathetic than she had a moment before. "Okay," Melanie said barely above a whisper. "But just this once, and don't you dare breathe a word to anybody."

Mona nodded, her face glowing with appreciation. "Thanks. You won't be sorry. I promise."

"Yo, Your Honor!"

Startled by the sound of Tony's voice, Katie jumped, causing the cold stream of water from the drinking fountain to splash her chin. She took a quick drink and wiped her chin with the back of her hand as she turned toward him. He had one eyebrow cocked, almost touching a strand of dark, wavy hair that tumbled across his forehead, and he was giving her his most irresistible smile.

"Yo, yourself," she answered playfully. No matter how hard she tried to act serious and totally cool around Tony, it never seemed to work.

"How's the crime-fighting business?" he asked as they made their way through the crowded halls toward the seventh-grade lockers.

"Bizarre," she said. "I think everybody's going bananas and doing weird things now that it's exam time. Teen Court has almost more cases than it can handle. Thank goodness you haven't been there for a while."

"Hey, what can I say?" he teased. "I'm just doing my part for a better Wacko Junior High."

Katie couldn't help laughing. Tony had a terrific sense of humor, and even though he was in trouble a lot, she loved having him for a boyfriend. He was very caring.

As soon as they reached her locker, Tony put his back firmly against the door so that she couldn't open it and crossed his arms over his chest.

"What are you doing?" she asked. "I have to get the books I need for my morning classes."

"You can get them," Tony said seriously. "Just as soon as I get a kiss."

Katie felt a blast of heat shoot up her face. *"Tony!"* she whispered hoarsely, and glanced around with embarrassment. *"Not here . . . in front of everyone."*

"What's wrong with here?" Tony challenged. "Nobody's looking." Reaching out, he grabbed her, pulling her close and wrapping his arms around her.

Katie made a weak attempt at resisting as his lips brushed her forehead. She started to argue further, but at that same instant she caught sight of Melanie, standing beside her own locker only a few feet away, watching with an amused look on her face. Beside Melanie stood Mona Vaughn, and she was looking at them, too.

"Talk about *boy crazy*," Melanie said. "Have you ever seen such a public display of affection?" She pretended to be talking to Mona, but she was speaking in such a loud voice that several kids at nearby lockers turned to stare at Katie and Tony.

Anger flashed through Katie like a windswept fire, and she pulled away from Tony, nervously smoothing her auburn hair with a hand. "What are you talking about?" she challenged. "We're just . . . just . . . horsing around. That's all."

"Su-u-u-ure you are," said Melanie. She turned away from Katie and then glanced back over her shoulder with a knowing smile.

"Sorry, Your Honor," Tony mumbled. "I didn't mean . . ."

"I know," Katie interrupted. "It wasn't your fault."

She watched Melanie and Mona move on down the hall and disappear in the crowd of students heading to class. Her anger was gone now, and she was left with a mixture of hurt and confusion. Of course she was always accusing Melanie of being boy crazy. And of course Melanie had a perfect right to tease her about Tony. Friends could always tease each other. But Melanie hadn't sounded as if she were teasing at all.

Katie put her arm through Tony's. The real difference between her and Melanie was that she was a one-guy girl, and he was a pretty terrific guy. She smiled up at him to show him she wasn't angry.

Beth was hurrying down the hall, trying to get to her English class before the last bell rang, when she spotted Jana coming toward her. Beth ducked into an empty classroom. She held her breath and crossed her fingers that Jana had not seen her, but luckily all the footsteps in the hall died away as the second bell sounded.

Now she would have to go to the office for a tardy slip, but at least that was better than facing Jana and telling her that she *still* hadn't had time to look through her collection of cassette tapes for the Bon Jovi tape that Jana had loaned her ages ago. Jana had asked her to bring it to school today, and Beth had promised that she would.

"I really meant to," she whispered to herself. "It's

just that I'm so busy. Nobody understands how much work all these dance committees are. And then there's homework . . ."

Beth sighed. She still couldn't help feeling guilty. Jana had been her very best friend practically forever. She hated breaking promises to Jana, and she also hated having to avoid coming face-to-face with her. But what else could she do? Beth asked herself for the millionth time. Jana just didn't seem to understand the predicament she was in. Maybe she could think up an excuse that Jana would believe before she saw her in the cafeteria at noon.

I'd better get my tardy slip and get to class, Beth thought, heading slowly out the empty classroom's door. She stepped into the silent hall expecting to scurry to the office without being seen, but instead she stopped in her tracks.

"Jana!" she gasped. "I mean . . . what are you . . ."

Jana stood facing Beth, her eyes swimming in tears. "I was right," she whispered. "It *was* you who ducked into that room."

Jana turned and dashed down the hall, leaving Beth fumbling for an explanation.

Christie took a container of milk and slid her tray along the track to the cash register. As the cashier totaled up her bill, she looked over her shoulder at The Fabulous Five's table. Melanie, Katie, Beth, and

Jana were already seated, and Christie could almost see a huge black cloud hanging over them as they each paid more attention to their lunches than each other.

"Two dollars and eighty-five cents," said the cashier. Christie paid, then headed for their table.

"Hi, everybody," she said as cheerfully as she could. Everyone murmured back hellos. "What's new?" she asked, glancing around the table.

"Well, some of us have been hiding out," said Jana, not taking her eyes off her cream cheese and jelly sandwich.

Christie saw Beth stir nervously in her seat and look furtively out of the corner of her eye at Jana. Something was definitely wrong between those two.

"Well, how are your tests going?" she asked Melanie, still searching for a way to get the conversation going. Usually, talking about tests brought out a cluster of moans, and then everyone started voicing complaints about their toughest teacher. Not this time, however,

"Can't we talk about something else?" asked Melanie. "I know school is *your* favorite subject, but tests depress me."

Christie could feel her face turning red and she looked away. I don't talk about school all the time, she thought indignantly. It's just that Melanie thinks the only conversations that count are the ones about boys.

Just then a sly expression slid across Melanie's

face. "We could talk about a big love scene I saw at the lockers," she said.

Katie's face turned almost as bright as her red hair. "That was *not* a big love scene," she protested. "Tony was just kidding around."

"Whoa!" said Melanie. "I wish I could get Shane or Scott to kid around like that."

Katie opened her mouth to respond, but Christie stopped her.

"Shhh!" she cautioned with a whisper. "Everyone's looking at us. Let's change the subject."

"Has Jon asked you to go to the dance with him?" Beth asked Christie.

"He did, but I told him I didn't think I wanted to go to the dance," responded Christie. The mouths of her four best friends dropped open simultaneously.

"*What?*" screeched Beth. "You're not going to the dance?"

Christie cringed at how loud Beth had said it. "Not so loud, *please*," she whispered again, glancing around to see who was looking. "There just isn't anyone I want to go with, so why should I go and have a boring time?"

"I can't believe it," said Melanie. "You may be the first junior high school girl in the history of the world who didn't want to go to a dance." Christie shrugged without commenting.

"Is something wrong?" asked Jana. "Are you feeling okay?"

"It couldn't be because your parents won't buy you a new dress," said Beth. "I know they would."

"Look, guys," Christie snapped. She was totally frustrated at their lack of understanding. "I just don't know of *anyone* I want to go to the dance with. It's *not* a crime, you know." Christie picked up her half-finished meal and stormed off to the tray-return line.

CHAPTER

3

*K*atie looked around the noisy study hall. Didn't anyone care that it was exam time? she wondered. Half the kids in the room were talking, and the other half were either passing notes or doodling in their notebooks as if all the information that they were supposed to be learning would magically pop into their heads the instant the test papers were passed out.

It was hard to concentrate with so much going on in the room, so she got up and went to the pencil sharpener. On the way back, she passed a table where, to her total surprise, Melanie sat with her head bent low, writing furiously in her notebook.

Katie stopped. She wanted to smooth things over between the two of them. Sinking into a vacant chair beside her friend, she said, "Way to go, Mel. What are you studying?"

Melanie looked up in surprise and then swallowed hard. "Oh, I'm just reviewing the history test we had yesterday," she mumbled.

Katie could tell from the tone of her voice that Melanie wasn't exactly telling the truth. If that weren't proof enough, Melanie tried to act casual and at the same time cover the notebook page with both hands.

Katie sighed, shaking her head. She should have known better than to think that Melanie was actually studying. "Okay, Melanie. What are you really doing? Writing a note to a boy?" she said, trying to sound cheerful.

She pulled the notebook out from under Melanie's hands and looked at the page, fully expecting to see a note beginning "Dear Shane" or "Dear Scott" or dear somebody else. Instead, the sheet was numbered down the left side from one to twenty-five, and beside each number was a word or phrase having something to do with American history.

"Whoops," Katie said, shrugging and chuckling at the same time. "I guess I was wrong. Sorry about that."

She handed the notebook back to Melanie, who still had a strange look on her face. Was she embarrassed because she was caught *studying*? Katie wondered in astonishment.

The two girls talked about other things for a few minutes more, but even after Katie had returned to her own table, she had the uneasy feeling that Melanie was hiding something.

When the bell rang ending the period, Katie scooped up her books and hurried to catch up with Melanie. As she closed in on Melanie, Mona Vaughn walked up and Melanie handed her a folded sheet of paper. It slipped out of Mona's hand, and as it fell to the floor, Katie could see that it was the page on which Melanie had been listing the answers to the history questions. Astounded, Katie dropped back and let the two girls walk on. She knew Mona had been absent the day before, and Mr. Naset would make her stay late to take the history test after class.

"I've had it!" Katie muttered aloud, and threw her pencil down on her desk so hard that it bounced and startled her cat, Libber, who had been curled up asleep in her lap. "I've got to do something."

She stood up, spilling Libber onto her bed, and began pacing the floor. Libber eyed her for a moment and then stretched lazily and settled into a new napping place on the corner of the bed.

Katie had been trying to study for her math test

ever since she had gotten home from school, but her mind refused to stay on the problems, jumping instead to the troubles within The Fabulous Five. Beth and Jana weren't speaking. Christie was carrying on as if the world would end if she didn't ace her exams and wasn't going to the school dance. And she and Melanie were not getting along, and maybe even worse, Melanie might be getting herself in trouble by giving Mona the answers to the history test. *How could she do such a thing?* The Fabulous Five's troubles were all just too much.

"Why don't you have a slumber party?" her mother had suggested when she complained about her friends at breakfast that morning. "It would give you a chance to talk out your problems," said Willie, giving Katie a sympathetic hug.

At the time it had seemed like a dumb idea. The five of them couldn't even get through lunch in the cafeteria without at least one argument erupting, so how could they possibly spend an entire night together in the same room without resorting to murder and mayhem?

Still, the more Katie thought about a slumber party, the better the idea sounded. Maybe Willie was right. After all, they *were* best friends, and they had always been able to handle any problems that came along when they really tried. She would have it on Friday night, she decided. And they would order in pizza and rent a movie, and later, snuggled in their sleeping bags, they would talk. Maybe, if she planned things right, it would be like old times again. Crossing her fingers and taking a deep breath, she raced downstairs to the phone.

Melanie had been so surprised by Katie's call the night before and her invitation to a slumber party that she had almost dropped the phone. Now as Melanie walked to school in the morning sunlight, she was still just as puzzled. She knew Katie was really steamed at her for the scene she had made at the lockers yesterday. Still, she thought, giggling, it served Katie right. Now she'll think twice before she calls me boy crazy.

Just inside the school grounds she saw Scott Daly leaning against a tree and watching her approach. "He's waiting for me," she whispered to herself. The thought made her tingle, and she walked faster.

"Hi, Scott. What's up?" she called out.

Scott moved forward to meet her, falling into step with her and tossing her an impish grin. "Do you realize that tomorrow night is Friday night?" he said mysteriously.

Melanie arched an eyebrow. "Of course. It's a big event that happens every week."

"Very good! For that terrific bit of wisdom you win the grand prize. Me and a movie tomorrow night!"

"Wow! That's the first time I ever won a grand prize," Melanie cried. But then her face fell.

"Whoops. I can't go. Katie's having a slumber party, and I promised her I'd be here."

"That's no problem. Why don't all five of you go to the movie?" Scott suggested. "You could all go to Katie's afterward. There'd still be plenty of time for your slumber party."

Melanie liked the idea, but Katie acted miffed when she suggested it at the fence a little while later. In fact, it seemed as if something was bugging Katie even before Melanie brought the idea up. "Go ahead and go to the movie if you'd rather be with Scott than The Fabulous Five," Katie said hotly. "That's what's the matter with everybody lately. Nobody has time for their *best friends* anymore."

"Forget it," muttered Melanie. "It was just a suggestion. You don't have to make a federal case out of it."

She found Scott at his locker and gave him the bad news.

"I guess I'll have to collect my grand prize some other time," she said. "Katie threw a fit. I don't know what the big deal is. She's been so grouchy lately, I bet she's inviting us over to feed us poison pizza."

Jana was just as apprehensive over the slumber party as Melanie was. She had always been the unofficial leader of The Fabulous Five, the one who could keep peace and hold everything together. But lately everyone had been so strung out that nothing she said or did had any effect. Still, Jana had to hand it to Katie. The slumber party might be just what they needed.

Friday evening she searched everywhere for her sleeping bag. In the tiny apartment she shared with her mother and Pink, there wasn't a lot of space to misplace things. It had been in the bottom of her mother's closet for ages, but now that Pink had moved in, his things filled the closet and hers had mysteriously disappeared.

"Mom," she said in an agitated voice when she found her mother in the living room, "did Pink move my sleeping bag without telling me? It's *supposed* to be in the bottom of your closet. That's where I always keep it. But it's not there now, and I need it for Katie's slumber party tonight."

Her mother thought a moment and then said, "Honey, you know that Pink had to have room for his clothes, and the closets in this apartment are pretty small. I don't remember what happened to it, but you might try looking in our storage space in the basement."

Jana stomped down to the basement and found her sleeping bag there, just as her mother had predicted, but it was under a stack of boxes, which took forever to move.

"Who does he think he is, moving my stuff around without asking?" she muttered as she headed for Katie's house twenty minutes late for the party and in an angry mood.

* * *

I wonder where Jana is? thought Beth. She was standing in the middle of Katie's living room, nervously tossing Jana's Bon Jovi tape from hand to hand and keeping an eye on the front door. She wished Jana would hurry up and get there so that she could give her the tape and get it over with. Maybe then Jana wouldn't be so angry with her for ducking into the empty classroom to avoid her.

Beth glanced around for something to keep herself occupied while she waited for Jana. The atmosphere in the room was tense, and Melanie was sitting on the sofa pretending to be absorbed in a magazine. Beth chuckled in spite of herself. Melanie only thought she was fooling everyone. Not only was the magazine some sort of technical journal for writers, but she was holding it upside down.

Just then the doorbell rang, and Beth jumped to open the door. It was Jana, with her sleeping bag under one arm and her backpack dangling from the other. The two stared at each other in awkward silence for a moment, and then Beth stepped aside so that Jana could enter.

"Here's your Bon Jovi tape." Beth said hurriedly, thrusting the cassette tape toward Jana and then realizing that Jana's hands were too full to take it. Instantly she felt like an idiot. How could I have done such a silly thing? she wondered.

"Umm. I'll hold it for you until you get your things settled," Beth said awkwardly.

Before Jana could reply, Katie and Christie entered the room from the kitchen, arguing.

"Whoever heard of someone's bringing their history book to a slumber party? Are you planning to be bored?" Katie demanded, and Beth had to admit that she had been wondering the same thing.

"Of course not," insisted Christie. "It's just that I have a humongous test coming up on Monday, and I still have three chapters to read and all my notes to go over. I thought maybe I could sneak a little time to read. Maybe after everybody goes to sleep."

"Well, don't let *us* disturb you," Katie said sarcastically.

Beth sat down on the opposite end of the sofa from Melanie and glanced at her watch. The slumber party was only thirty minutes old, but it seemed like a year. How could they possibly spend the entire night together?

Next Katie ordered two superdeluxe pizzas with everything on them, which took forever to get there and when they did, were cold. By this time, Beth was starting to panic. She had to think of something to lighten up the mood.

"At least we have a movie to watch," she chirped. "You did stop by the video rental store and get a movie, didn't you, Katie?"

Katie's mouth was full of cold pizza so she only nodded.

"I hope you got *Ghostbusters* or *Ghostbusters II*," Beth said. "Those movies are so wild and so funny."

Katie wrinkled her nose in disgust. "Are you kidding? Those movies are disgusting. I got a really good movie. *Gorillas in the Mist*. It's terrific."

Beth groaned and then said in a monotone voice, "I know. I already saw it."

"Well, at least it has more to it than green slime," Katie retorted. "It's about a woman who sees a problem and *does* something about it."

"But it's so serious and so sad," Beth argued. "It's not the kind of movie that you rent for a slumber party. This night's supposed to be fun, remember?"

No one else said anything, but Beth could tell from the expressions on their faces that Melanie, Christie, and Jana were just as miserable as she was. Silently they lined up in the living room to glumly watch *Gorillas in the Mist*. Katie made popcorn, but hardly anyone touched it. Finally the movie was over, and they trudged up to Katie's room for the night.

Christie waited until no one was looking and then sneaked her history book into her sleeping bag. This evening was turning out to be a total disaster just as she had known it would, but maybe she could get a little studying done when everyone else went to sleep, no matter what Katie thought about the idea. She had even brought a tiny flashlight, planning to zip herself into her sleeping bag and turn it on without disturbing anyone else.

Around the room the others were getting ready for bed without the usual chatter that always accompanied one of The Fabulous Five's slumber parties. Christie felt a lump forming in her throat. She missed things the way they used to be, but it was time for her friends to grow up a little and realize how serious life really was.

It was Melanie who broke the silence a few minutes later. "Scott says that he really misses me when I don't show up at Bumpers or the movie or someplace where he usually sees me," she said with a sigh, and then snuggled into her pink and white sleeping bag. "Just think, this whole evening while we've been watching that *dumb* movie and eating *cold* pizza, Scott has been all alone in the movie theater, pining away because I'm not there."

"Oh, Melanie. You're too much," groaned Katie, falling back onto her pillow. "You're the most gullible person I've ever met. You believe anything Scott or anybody else tells you."

"I am *not* gullible, Katie Shannon," Melanie retorted.

"Oh, no?" challenged Katie. "Don't tell me that you wouldn't do almost anything someone asks you to, like even helping with tests."

Melanie's face froze, and she stared at Katie with disbelief in her eyes.

"Gosh, Katie," said Christie. "You should try to

be more open-minded about things. Maybe Scott's telling the truth. And even if he isn't, why should it matter to you?"

"Humpf," snorted Katie. "It's obvious that you don't know much about human nature. Especially *boys'* nature. I have to deal with it all the time in Teen Court. The kids who come to court are either innocent or guilty, and I have to figure out which one. I have to understand human nature to be able to be fair."

"Speaking of boys," said Jana, looking very serious, "Funny told me something I need to pass on to you, Katie." She hesitated before continuing, then taking in a deep breath, she said, "Tammy Lucero says she has seen Tony over at Shawnie Pendergast's house a lot lately."

Katie looked at her with amazement. *"Tammy said that?* You know what kind of a gossip Tammy is, and she's always trying to make trouble for us. I'm surprised you think there could be any truth to it."

Jana shifted uncomfortably. "I detoured down her street Monday on the way home from school, and Tony's bike *was* in front of Shawnie's. I'm sorry," she said in a small voice.

"So much for knowing human nature," said Christie.

"Christie," Melanie called from across the room. "What I can never understand is how you can be so uptight about everything all the time. You don't have any tests until Monday. Why don't you relax tonight and study tomorrow?"

"I am relaxed," Christie insisted. "But you know I get a lot of pressure from my parents to get straight A's. I guess you'd just have to get the kind of pressure I get to understand."

Melanie crossed her eyes to show everyone that she thought Christie's remarks about pressure were silly. It broke the tension, and they all giggled, including Christie.

Everyone was quiet for the next moment or two, and then suddenly Beth jumped to her feet with a big smile on her face. "Come on, Melanie. Help me teach everybody some new cheers. That should liven things up."

Melanie screwed up her face. "Do cheers? At this time of night? You've got to be kidding."

"I'm not kidding," Beth said earnestly. "It'll be fun. Come on."

Melanie flopped onto her back and stared at the ceiling. Christie could tell that leading cheers was the last thing in the world she felt like doing.

Christie was glad. For once Melanie was using good sense. Turning to Beth, Christie couldn't resist remarking, "It would be great if you could be a little quieter and less dramatic some of the time. People would take you seriously more often."

Anger flickered on Beth's face for an instant and then disappeared. "Christie," she said patiently, "not everyone is as quiet and conservative as you are. It's just my personality to be dramatic. I guess you can't understand that."

Christie shrugged and played with the zipper on her sleeping bag. Beth's right about that, she thought. I'll never understand how anyone can be the way she is, trying to be the center of attention all the time and dressing like somebody out of a science fiction movie.

But Beth wasn't finished talking yet. "And you, Jana," she continued, "you gripe all the time about Pink and how he's taking over your space. You ought to live with two brothers and two sisters. Then you'd *really* have something to gripe about. Being the middle child is definitely no fun."

Jana looked hurt. "But I don't gripe all the time," she protested. "You don't understand me at all."

"Yes, you do," insisted Beth. "You gripe all the time. Believe me, I'm your best friend. I ought to know."

Christie got slowly to her feet. "Look, guys," she began. "We're all in bad moods tonight. In fact we've been in bad moods for days, and I think we should stop picking on each other before something awful happens. We're all best friends, remember? And we—"

Christie's words were interrupted by a knock on the bedroom door.

Katie held up her hand for quiet. "Mom? Is that you? Come on in."

Willie Shannon opened the door just far enough

to stick her head into the room. "I hate to ask this, girls," she began, "but would you mind cooling it for now? It's getting late, and we all need to get some sleep."

"Gosh, Mrs. Shannon, we're sorry," said Jana. "We didn't mean to keep you awake."

"Right," said Christie. "We didn't realize it was so late."

"Thanks," said Willie. "You're all . . . well, you're *fabulous*," she said with a little laugh. "I'll see you in the morning."

The lights went out, and the room grew quiet. Melanie and Beth turned onto their right sides and drew their knees up. Katie punched her pillow and sprawled out on her stomach. Christie ran her hand over the history book inside her sleeping bag and decided to wait until morning to read it, and Jana scooted down until her sleeping bag covered her head.

Each of them was feeling miserable and misunderstood. And as each fell asleep, she began dreaming. . . .

CHAPTER

4

"Come on, girls. Rise and shine," called Willie. "I hate to give you the bad news, but it's time to get up and head for home."

Opening one eye, Melanie squinted at her watch: 10:43. How could she be so sleepy when it was that late? Then she remembered the slumber party and Mrs. Shannon's asking them to go to sleep. Melanie groaned. Why had Katie's mother waited until so late? Why hadn't she come by earlier?

She could hear the rest of The Fabulous Five stirring, and she stretched as far as she could, trying to wake up her entire body. That's funny, she thought. My legs feel too long. If it hadn't taken too much energy, she would have laughed at the thought. That's silly, she told herself. They're *my* legs.

She grumbled a sleepy hello to her friends, who looked just as out of it as she felt, and started to roll up her sleeping bag. Then she remembered the conversation The Fabulous Five had been having just before they went to sleep and she felt angry all over again. I am not gullible, she told herself emphatically. Why doesn't anyone understand? Melanie slipped out of the oversize T-shirt she wore as a nightgown, pulled on her powder-blue sweats, and grabbed her sleeping bag, heading out of Katie's room without another word. She didn't want to talk to anyone. She just wanted to go home.

"Got time for some breakfast?" Willie asked cheerfully when Melanie reached the kitchen.

"Thanks, but I just want to go home and get back to sleep. Thanks for everything, Mrs. Shannon, and I hope we didn't keep you up too late," she called as she rushed on out the back door.

The cool air made her feel a little better, but she was still in a sleepy stupor when she opened her own front door and went inside.

"Morning, sweetheart," her father called from the family room. "Have a good time?"

"Uh-huh. But boy, am I beat. I'm going up to my room and crash. See you later."

Melanie started up the stairs, dragging her sleeping bag behind her. Suddenly she stopped midway up and looked around.

"This is Christie's house," she muttered under her breath. "And the father I just said good morning to was Christie's father. He acted as if I were Christie. Why didn't he notice that I'm Melanie?"

She looked down at her legs. They *were* too long. And the powder-blue sweat suit she was wearing was the one Christie had been wearing the night before.

Melanie swallowed hard, trying to fight down the wad of panic that was gathering in her throat. Leaving the sleeping bag on the stairs, she raced to Christie's room and looked in the dresser mirror. The face that looked back at her belonged to Christie Winchell, and the body in the blue sweats was tall and thin with very long legs.

"Oh, my gosh!" she gasped. Then she pulled a strand of hair out in front of her face and looked at it. It was blond instead of the reddish-brown that it should be.

Looking back into the mirror, she studied the face. It *was* Christie's face, and she was in Christie's body.

"But that can't be," she whispered in astonishment. "I'm Melanie. Melanie Edwards."

Backing up slowly, she sat down on Christie's bed. She was filled with a strange dread as she picked up the receiver of the phone on Christie's night stand, dialing her own number.

It rang twice, and then a familiar voice said, "Hello. Edwards residence. Melanie speaking."

*   *   *

Katie was in no mood for conversation when she left the slumber party and headed for home. Why was it that her friends were always picking on Tony? she wondered as she hoisted her sleeping bag onto her shoulder and stomped down the street. Just because he got into trouble now and then was no reason always to assume the worst. There had to be an explanation about Tony and Shawnie, and it was only fair to let him tell her what it was.

She was reaching for the knob on her front door when suddenly the door jerked open from the inside and Jeffy sprang at her, yelling, "*Ya!* You're home! Now you can play Nintendo with me. Ya! Ya!"

"Forget it, squirt," she snapped. "I've been up all night, and I'm in no mood for video games."

Jeffy grabbed her sleeve and pulled hard. "Come on, Mel. Pleeeeease. I'll let you be first."

"Not now, Jeffy," Katie insisted. "Maybe later. Okay?"

Jeffy stuck out his lower lip and looked up at her with pleading eyes, but she stood her ground. "Later. Got it?"

Heading into the deserted kitchen, Katie opened the refrigerator and pulled out a carton of milk and then took a glass out of the cabinet. She was heading for bed, and a glass of milk would keep the hungries away until she woke up. She had already started pouring the milk when an odd feeling came over her. Why had Jeffy called her Mel? She was Katie, not Melanie. And what was she doing in Melanie's house in the first place? The slumber party had been held at her own house. Why hadn't she stayed there? Her eyes widened in astonishment as she looked around the room. It *was* Melanie's house. What on earth was going on? It was as if she had stepped into the Twilight Zone.

Something cold splashed on her hand, and she looked down to see the milk overflowing the glass and pouring onto the floor like a waterfall. Racing to the sink, she set down the carton and glass and frantically looked around for a towel.

"I've got to wipe up this mess before Mrs. Edwards sees it and gets mad," she mumbled to herself. Jerking herself upright, she glanced furtively toward the door. "Before she sees *me* and wants to know why I'm here instead of Melanie."

Just then the phone rang, further jangling her nerves. Out of habit she grabbed it and was startled to hear herself say, "Hello. Edwards residence. Melanie speaking."

Oh, no! That's wrong! I'm Katie Shannon! she wanted to shout, but the words refused to come out, and on the other end of the line, the caller hung up.

Jana felt like a zombie. Her head throbbed, and her eyes felt as if she had been up for days instead of half the night. She pulled the corner of the sleeping bag over her face to keep out the light and listened to her friends getting dressed to go home. She knew that she should get up and at least talk to them, since she was the hostess, but she was just too tired. Besides, she was still smarting over the things Beth had said to her the night before. As much as making her angry, it had hurt to think that her very best friend misunderstood her so badly.

"Katie," she heard Beth whisper from somewhere near the top of her sleeping bag. "Katie, are you awake?"

If I fake being asleep, maybe she'll go away and leave me alone, thought Jana. Maybe they all will.

Moments later the room was still, and Jana slowly wiggled her way out of her sleeping bag and sat up. Everyone was gone except Libber. The sleek yellow cat was sitting near the bedroom door, meticulously washing a paw. Under Jana's steady gaze Libber stopped washing and fixed her golden eyes on Jana. Then she tiptoed across the room and snuggled into Jana's lap, purring softly.

Jana smiled and stroked Libber's head. "At least you still like me," she said as Libber revved up her purr until it sounded like a souped-up car getting ready for a race.

Suddenly Jana's nose started to twitch. She looked down at the sleeping cat in her lap and sighed. How could I have forgotten? she thought. I can't hold Libber in my lap when I have a cold. I'm allergic to cats, and when I have a cold, they make me twice as miserable. But she had remembered too late.

"Ah-ah-ah-*choo*!"

Libber's ears pricked straight up, and she shot across the room and out the door like a furry, yellow comet.

Jana tried to call out to her and tell her it was okay, but another sneeze was tickling her nose. "Ah-choo!" And another. "Ah-choo!" And another and another. "Ah-choo! Ah-choo!"

She jumped out of the sleeping bag and headed straight for the tissue box in the bathroom, nearly colliding with Willie Shannon in the hall.

"Katie, you sound awful," exclaimed Mrs. Shannon. "I think you're coming down with something." With that, Katie's mother put a hand on Jana's forehead. "Well, at least you don't feel feverish."

"It's Libber," Jana started to explain. "I'm allerg-a-a-a-*choo*!"

"Now don't argue with me, sweetheart," said Willie, taking Jana by the arm and steering her toward the bedroom. "This is one time when mother knows best. You climb into bed, and I'll bring you some tissues and some cold medicine."

Jana opened her mouth to protest, but Katie's mother held up a hand for silence. "I'll take no nonsense about this. I want you to stay right there until you're well, and that's final."

Jana blew her nose loudly and then looked around Katie's room in bewildered silence. This can't be happening, she told herself. Not only is Katie Shannon's mother holding me prisoner in this bedroom, but she thinks that I'm Katie!

* * *

Beth slipped between the cool sheets, grateful to be back in her own bed again. She planned to sleep the rest of the day and maybe not even get up until tomorrow, except perhaps to eat.

She turned on her side and closed her eyes, thinking that the house was amazingly quiet for a Saturday morning. Usually Brian's stereo music was rocking the house off its foundation. Maybe he's at someone else's house, rocking their house off its foundation, she thought hopefully. Brittany wasn't out in the hall talking on the phone, either. That was odd. Her older sister spent most of her waking moments on the telephone. Beth strained, listening to the unusual stillness.

Her younger brother, Todd, wasn't bouncing his basketball on the driveway under her window, and Alicia wasn't tearing around the house shouting "Agafa! Agafa!" as she chased the family's old English sheepdog, Agatha, through the rooms upsetting everything that wasn't nailed down.

"How can I possibly go to sleep with all of this quiet?" she thought out loud.

She turned onto her other side and lay that way for a moment. Then she stretched out on her back and gazed at the ceiling while she thought about the slumber party the night before.

"Who does Christie think she is, calling me loud and obnoxious?" Beth said, speaking the words louder than she had meant to. "Well, she didn't exactly say I was *loud* or *obnoxious*," she whispered. "But that's what she meant."

The memory of Christie's criticism made her more restless than ever, and before long she had the sheet tangled around herself like a straitjacket.

"Where's Agatha?" she muttered. "She's always here when I need someone to talk to."

Beth got out of bed and opened the door a crack. She could see down the hall and into a little bit of the living room where what seemed to be her mother's feet were sticking out in front of the sofa. Opening the door far enough to squeeze out, Beth got down on her hands and knees. Maybe she could find Agatha without attracting her mother's attention, and then the two of them could sneak back into the bedroom. If her mother saw that she was awake, she would surely find chores for Beth to do.

"Agatha," Beth whispered as she crawled along. "Agatha! Where are you?"

She crawled past the bathroom, scarcely glancing inside since the bathroom was so small and Agatha was so large.

"Here, Agatha," she called again.

Just then she heard footsteps coming toward her, and suddenly the feet that had been sticking out in front of the sofa only an instant before were standing right before her.

"Jana, what on earth are you doing?" asked Mrs.

Pinkerton. "Why are you crawling around on your hands and knees?"

Beth looked up and was too flabbergasted to speak for a moment. Mrs. Pinkerton had called her Jana. Couldn't she see that she was Jana's best friend, Beth Barry?

When Beth didn't answer, Mrs. Pinkerton sighed impatiently. "I asked you a question, honey. Why don't you answer?"

"I . . . I was just calling Agatha. That's all."

"Agatha?" Jana's mother looked puzzled. "Isn't that the name of Beth's dog? Why on earth would Beth Barry's dog be in our apartment?" Then she laughed and added, "It's hardly big enough for the three of us, much less an old English sheepdog."

Beth sat back on her haunches dog style and looked up at Mrs. Pinkerton. Then she looked around at the narrow hallway leading into the tiny living room of the apartment as she began understanding why things were so quiet. She wasn't at home. She was at Jana's. But why? And why did Mrs. Pinkerton insist on calling her Jana? She must need her glasses changed, Beth thought.

Getting slowly to her feet, Beth stepped closer to Mrs. Pinkerton, hoping that a better look at Beth would tell Jana's mother who Beth really was.

Just then Pink came out of the kitchen and joined them. Pink was the nickname everyone used for Wallace Pinkerton, and he was Jana's stepfather.

Beth liked him a lot, so she smiled and said, "Hi, Pink. How are you doing?"

"Good morning, Jana," he replied pleasantly. "I'm fine, but you look a little sleepy."

He thinks I'm Jana, too! Beth wanted to explain, but she couldn't. Her lips had turned to cement and were stuck too tightly together for her to speak a word. She stared at Jana's parents for a moment and then nodded and headed back to bed.

What Christie wanted most in the world was a shower. Sleep could wait. She closed the bathroom door tightly behind her and turned on the water. While it warmed, she stripped off her clothes and searched the linen closet for her favorite shampoo. It wasn't there.

That's funny, she thought. I could have sworn that I opened a new bottle yesterday. But strangely, there were seven kinds of shampoo in the top shelf and none of them were hers. Shrugging, she grabbed one of the others and stepped into the shower. She would worry about the great shampoo mystery later when she wasn't so sleepy.

The warm water felt wonderful as it caressed her shoulders and ran down her body. She stood there for a moment, not moving, just enjoying the refreshing feel of the water. Finally she grabbed the shampoo and massaged a handful into her hair and scalp.

She frowned. Her hair felt shorter than usual. It must be this new shampoo, she mused.

Christie didn't know how long she stood in the shower. It didn't matter, she told herself. Her parents would have showered ages ago, and she was the only one of the Winchells' three children who still lived at home. That meant she had loads of privacy, which was exactly the way she liked it.

She sighed as she turned off the water and wrapped her hair in a towel, thinking that there was only one thing spoiling what would otherwise have been a perfect morning. She had just remembered the slumber party and Melanie's telling her to loosen up. What a crummy thing to say to a best friend. Still, she mused, she couldn't really expect Melanie to understand.

"But it would be nice if she would *try*," Christie said out loud.

She glanced toward the mirror to see if her eyes looked red from lack of sleep, but the steam from the shower had completely fogged it over. Shrugging, she wrapped a towel around herself and headed for her room.

The instant she stepped into the hall she froze.

"It's about time you got out of there," Brian Barry said angrily. "You know there's a time limit on the bathroom. And take the Silly Putty out of your ears. I've pounded my knuckles to a pulp trying to get your attention."

Christie clutched her towel in horror. Here she was coming out of the bathroom practically naked, and Beth Barry's older brother was waiting in the hall.

"Well," he snapped, "are you going to stand there blocking the door all day?"

"I . . . bu . . . you . . ." Christie stammered to find the words to ask him what he was doing there and why he was talking to her as if she were Beth, but the words wouldn't come. And why did this hallway look like Beth's hall? And now that she thought of it, why did the bathroom look like the one at Beth's house? Suddenly she realized how skimpy her towel was. It hardly covered anything. Pulling it tighter around her, she dashed down the hall toward her room.

CHAPTER

5

*M*elanie sat on the edge of Christie's bed and thought about her predicament. She didn't know how it had happened, but she was in Christie's body. It was a fact, and there didn't seem to be anything she could do about it.

She got up and went to the mirror again. Maybe seeing Christie's image in the mirror had been her imagination, she thought hopefully. Everyone was always saying that she had a vivid imagination. But no, Christie's face was still looking back at her. Was it a trick? she asked herself. Magicians did tricks with mirrors. Maybe someone had pasted Christie's picture to the mirror so that she would be fooled.

Slowly she raised an index finger to touch her nose. Christie in the mirror did the same thing at exactly the same time. This was no trick. At least, no trick with mirrors.

"I know," Melanie whispered. "I'll go downstairs and talk to Christie's parents. Oh, panic! What if they won't believe me? I'll *make* them believe me, and then I'll ask them to help me get my old body back. I know they'll do it. They won't want a *fake* Christie around all the time."

Melanie ran a brush through her long blond hair so that it would look as neat as Christie always kept it and checked the pale blue sweat suit for dirt or wrinkles. Christie never wore anything with a wrinkle or a spot of dirt on it. She passed inspection and was just about to go into the hall when she heard Mrs. Winchell calling Christie.

"Christie. Why on earth did you leave your sleeping bag in the middle of the stairway? Someone could trip over it."

"Sorry, Mom. I'll get it right now," she called back, startled at how much her voice sounded like Christie's.

She hurried out and grabbed the bag under Mrs. Winchell's watchful gaze. This was definitely not the time to tell her that the Christie she was scolding was actually Melanie Edwards, Melanie thought.

"It isn't like you to be so careless," said Christie's mother a little more kindly. "You must be extra-tired from the slumber party last night."

Melanie nodded. Whew, she thought, maybe she'll send me back to bed, and I can have more time to think.

"Why don't you rest awhile," said Mrs. Winchell as if on cue. "I'll wake you in an hour, and then we can go over this list of history questions you asked me to help you review."

Melanie blinked in astonishment. History questions? "Okay, Mom," she said quickly, and streaked back to Christie's room. Closing the door behind herself, she sank to the floor.

"I don't know the first thing about the history class that Christie's taking. It's an *honors* class, and only brains like Christie take it in seventh grade."

She stood up and raced to the mirror again. "Please. Oh, please, don't be Christie anymore," she cried. "Be *Melanie*!" But the face that looked back at her was still Christie's.

Melanie turned away from the mirror and began rummaging through Christie's sleeping bag, looking for her history book. What chapters would the test be on? Could she possibly cram almost an entire semester of honors history into one hour of studying? Of course not! But she had to in order to get on Mrs. Winchell's good side, Melanie reasoned. Only then could she tell Christie's mother who she really was.

Melanie located a heavy lump in the middle of the bedroll and extracted a large gray history book, a tiny flashlight, and a small spiral notebook.

"Bingo!" she cried, jumping up and down with excitement. "I've found it! I've found it!"

But her excitement passed quickly as she thumbed through the big textbook. The print was small, and most of the pictures were of stern-looking kings or battles between armies on horseback. "Dullsville," she muttered in disgust. And there was no way to tell which chapter Christie was reading. She was too neat to turn down the corner of a page to mark her place, and if she had put a bookmark in, it had fallen out. It would be just like her to memorize the page she was on, thought Melanie.

Then she remembered the notebook. To her immense relief it was Christie's assignment notebook, and on the last page of writing she had written: *Hist. assgn., read Chs. 19–20. Review quests Ch. 18.*

Melanie almost collapsed with relief. Now, at least, she knew what to study. Then she looked at her watch. Eeek! she thought. I've wasted fifteen minutes finding the assignment. That means I only have forty-five minutes left to become a genius!

Christie closed Beth's bedroom door and sank to her knees, still clutching the towel around herself. "This is the most bizarre thing that has ever happened to me," she said half aloud. "They think I'm Beth. They *actually* think I'm Beth."

Heat crept up her neck and spread over her face as she remembered facing Brian in the hall wearing nothing but a towel. How can I ever look at him again? she thought.

"Bethy! Bethy! Let me in!" Alicia cried from the hall. "Todd's teasing me, and he won't leave me alone."

"Alicia, Todd, Brian. This place is a madhouse," Christie muttered. Then she remembered that they all thought she was Beth and that Alicia might simply come crashing in, so she yelled, "Just a minute, Alicia. I'm not dressed."

"Well, *hurry*," shouted Alicia, and Christie could hear tears in her voice.

Maybe Alicia could help her, Christie thought. If anyone could tell that she wasn't Beth, surely Alicia could. Not only that, Alicia was young enough to believe in Santa Claus and the Easter Bunny and probably even fairies and elves, so she would surely believe what had happened to Christie. Then Alicia could help her convince Beth's parents, and maybe, just maybe, together they could find a way to turn her back into who she really was—Christie Winchell.

Christie raced to the bureau and opened the top drawer. Inside was a jumble of multicolored bras and panties. Christie reached out to grab the nearest bra, but her hand stopped in midair. This was Beth's underwear. How could she possible wear somebody else's bra? Or panties? She stared into the drawer for a moment as if it were full of snakes. But what choice did she have?

"I'll explain to Beth," she muttered, "and take them home and wash them before I give them back."

Next she went to the closet and was hit by a tidal wave of color. Purple-and-orange plaid. Electric green with huge watermelon polka dots. Black and white diagonal stripes.

Christie closed her eyes and pictured her own closet filled with soft hues of beige and brown, lots of pale blue to complement her blond hair and eyes, and tons of pinks and soft greens.

"I can't possibly wear any of this crazy stuff," she whispered, opening her eyes again. "But I have to," she reminded herself. "As least as long as everyone thinks that I'm Beth."

Christie went through the closet hanger by hanger, looking for the least-wild outfit, but nothing qualified. They were all wild. She put one hand over her eyes and held out the other hand, vowing to wear whatever it touched, no matter what.

"Oh, no," she moaned as she pulled out a hanger and opened her eyes. She had picked an oversize black sweatshirt covered with silver lightning bolts. On the hanger underneath were silver lamé stretch pants. Christie gritted her teeth and put on the outfit.

Taking a deep breath, she went to the door and called, "Okay, Alicia. You can come in now."

Beth sat on the floor in Jana's room, staring at the door and listening to the quiet. This is too much, she thought. Why doesn't somebody drop something or turn up the television or *something*? How could a person even think in all this quiet? And think was exactly what she needed to do.

She had gone over the events of last night's slumber party for the millionth time and always came to the same conclusion. She had criticized Jana for griping so much about her life now that she had a stepfather, and here she was *living* Jana's life instead of her own.

"This can't be happening! It's impossible!" she whispered, and then looked around in fright. Even the tiniest whisper seemed to echo in the silent room. Suddenly she was filled with longing for Brian's stereo music, for Agatha's bark, for Todd's basketball thumping on the driveway outside her window, and even for Brittany's long-winded conversations on the phone. All this quiet just wasn't normal.

The sudden ring of the telephone, sounding as loud as a siren's blast in the silent apartment, startled her so much that she jumped to her feet. Maybe it was the real Jana, calling to say that she was on her way home, Beth thought.

But her hope was shattered the next instant when she heard Mrs. Pinkerton call, "Jana, it's for you."

Beth hesitated a moment and then went to answer the phone. It still might be Jana, she reasoned. Maybe she knows what happened to me and she wants to help me get back to being myself. Or maybe she's mad at me for impersonating her. In either case, it would be terrific to talk to someone who understood.

The telephone was in the kitchen, and the first thing she noticed when she picked the receiver up off the counter was that she had an audience. Mrs. Pinkerton was putting away groceries and Pink was sitting at the kitchen table going through the day's mail. They looked busy, but they couldn't help overhearing her conversation in the tiny room.

Beth bit her lower lip and put the receiver to her ear. "Hello?" she said nervously.

"Hi, Jana. How was the slumber party last night?"

Beth froze. It was Randy Kirwan, Jana's boyfriend, and he thought he was talking to Jana.

"Okay," she answered. "Fun, actually," she added, trying to decide what Jana would say. "Katie rented a movie and we had pizza, and then . . . then we talked." She bit her lower lip again. Would he really believe she was Jana?

Across the room Jana's mother looked at Beth and smiled approvingly. She's listening, Beth thought, getting panicky. Nobody ever listened to her conversations at home. They were all too busy. Besides, it was usually too noisy to hear.

Randy was talking again. Beth turned her attention back to him and caught the last half of a sentence: ". . . so I thought I'd check and see what time you wanted me to come over tonight."

"Tonight?" Beth squeaked.

"Sure," Randy said, sounding puzzled. "Don't you remember? When you told me about Katie's slumber party, you said we could get together tonight instead. Then you suggested that I rent a movie and come over there."

"Right," said Beth nervously. "I remember."

"Great," said Randy. "How does six-thirty sound?"

"It sounds terrific. I'll see you then." Beth's hand was shaking when she hung up the phone. It couldn't be happening, but it was. She had a date with her best friend's boyfriend.

Jana tugged one of the tissues out of the box and wiped away a tear that was rolling down her face. She didn't want to be Katie. And she certainly didn't want to be shut up in Katie's bedroom and treated like an invalid. She wanted to go home.

But how could she? Willie Shannon was convinced that she was Katie, and one look in the mirror on Katie's dresser had told Jana why. Jana looked like Katie, all right. She had the same fiery-red hair. The small, slim body. Even the green eyes were like Katie's. But what had happened to her real body? The body of Jana Morgan?

The more she thought about that, the more she felt like crying. "I want my own body back," she sobbed, falling back on the pillows.

Her lack of sleep the night before caught up with her, and she drifted off to sleep a little while later only to wake up to the sound of a knock on the door.

"It's me, honey," called Willie. "I've made you some chicken noodle soup. May I come in?"

"Sure," said Jana, who realized suddenly that she hadn't eaten since the cold pizza the night before.

She scooted up to a sitting position as Katie's mother entered the room and set a tray with little legs across her lap.

"I hated to wake you," said Willie. "But it's getting late, and I knew you needed some nourishment."

"Thanks," Jana said shyly. "It smells delicious."

Willie looked surprised. "I'm glad you think so," she said. "I know you don't like chicken noodle soup, but it's all I have in the house."

Whoops, thought Jana. I didn't know that Katie doesn't like chicken noodle soup. She eyed Willie nervously. Maybe she should explain to Katie's mother why the soup smelled so good to her. She could tell Willie that she was really Jana and that Jana loved chicken noodle soup.

But she'd never believe me, Jana thought sadly. Never in a million years. In fact, she might think I'd flipped and take me to see a doctor. A shrink! Then I would really be in trouble.

Her thoughts were interrupted by Willie, who reached out to feel her forehead. "Still no fever," she said cheerfully. "A good night's rest and you'll be fine in the morning. Just put the tray in the hall when you're finished, and I'll see you at breakfast." With that Willie bent over and planted a kiss on her forehead before leaving the room.

Long shadows were crisscrossing the room as Jana gobbled up the delicious soup. Then she looked at the clock on Katie's bedside table and gasped. Five-thirty in the afternoon.

"I've been gone most of the day," she said aloud. "Mom must be getting worried. Maybe I should call her and tell her I'm okay." It only took an instant to decide against that. There was no phone upstairs in the Shannon house, and Willie might see her if she went down to the kitchen.

Slowly another idea began forming. There was a tree outside Katie's second-floor window. She and Katie had climbed it when they were younger. They had actually used it to sneak up to Katie's room, so why couldn't she use it to sneak out and go home?

Jana changed quickly into a pair of Katie's jeans and a sweater. At five minutes to six she raised the window and slipped out into the branches of the tree.

Katie unrolled a handful of paper towels and began wiping the spilled milk off of the Edwardses' kitchen floor. Her mind was whirling. Why had she answered the phone, "Hello. Edwards residence. Melanie speaking"? She wasn't Melanie. She was

Katie. But even Jeffy had thought she was Melanie.
There has to be a logical explanation for all this, she
told herself. But what was it?

"Oh, Melanie. You're home from the slumber
party," said Mrs. Edwards, coming into the kitchen.
"Did you girls have fun?"

Katie dabbed up the last drop of milk and stood
up, facing Melanie's mother. She was hoping that
Mrs. Edwards would notice the mistake she was
making when she got a good look at Katie's face.

"You don't have to answer that one," Mrs. Edwards said, and chuckled. "Your red, puffy eyes do
it for you. You girls must have talked all night."

Katie was flabbergasted. Was it possible that she
did look like Melanie? After all, she had come to
Melanie's house instead of going to her own.

Melanie's mother was still looking at her as if she
expected conversation.

"Yeah, we talked until Mrs. Shannon asked us to
stop," she admitted.

"Poor Willie," Mrs. Edwards exclaimed, and
turned away, busying herself at the kitchen sink.

The wheels were turning in Katie's mind as she
stared at Mrs. Edwards's back. *She* knew who she
was. She was Katie, not Melanie. The logical thing
to do was to talk to Melanie's parents, beginning
with Mrs. Edwards, and explain the whole thing the
best way she could. She would simply tell them that
she had gone to sleep in her own body and awakened
this morning in Melanie's. She would also tell them

that she didn't know how such a freaky thing happened or what to do about it and ask them to call the police or *someone* who could straighten the whole thing out. She felt sure they would help her since she knew they would want to get the real Melanie back.

Katie frowned. She hadn't thought about that part of it. Is Melanie at my house? Pretending to be me? Katie snapped to attention. This is urgent, she thought. I have to talk to Mrs. Edwards right now.

CHAPTER

6

It was no trouble scrambling down the tree, and Jana squatted low and duck-walked beneath the windows and across the yard to the safety of the sidewalk. Then she stood up and dashed madly toward home.

She had a pain in her side from running when she reached her apartment building, and she stopped in the doorway to let the pain subside and her breathing get back to normal.

"Rats!" she exclaimed as she dug in Katie's jeans pocket. "My key would be in my own clothes, not Katie's. I guess I'll have to ring the bell."

Jana climbed the stairs and stopped in front of her

apartment door. It felt a little weird to be ringing her own doorbell, but not half as weird as what had been going on since she woke up this morning. But as soon as she got inside, she would be home, and she could talk to her mother, and everything would be all right again.

She pushed the buzzer and waited, dancing around on the balls of her feet with excitement. Only a few seconds went by until the door swung open and her mother stood smiling at her.

"Katie, what a pleasant surprise," her mother said. "Jana didn't mention anything about your coming over, but come on in. I'm sure she'll be glad to see you."

Jana stared at her mother in horror. Her worst nightmare had just come true. Her own mother didn't know who she was! Surely the other Jana, whoever she was, would understand. She gave her mother a bewildered look and hurried down the hall to her room, knocking softly on the door.

"Who is it?" came a voice from inside.

"Katie."

Jana gasped. The word had come out involuntarily. She had tried her best to say Jana. "I know I did," she whispered to herself.

Suddenly the door opened and she found herself staring into the face of another Jana. "Come on in," the new Jana said.

Jana stepped awkwardly into the room. The new Jana was standing before the dresser mirror brushing her hair, and she looked as if she were getting ready to go somewhere. Not only that, the real Jana thought angrily, she's wearing my new denim jumper! I've been saving it for my next date with Randy. What's going on here?

"Going out?" the real Jana asked.

The new Jana shook her head. "Randy's coming over."

The real Jana gasped. Randy! How could she have forgotten their plans for this evening? And what was she going to do? She couldn't let this fake have a date with *her* boyfriend! Wait until I tell her off, she thought angrily. But when she started to speak, she was amazed at what came out. "Tony asked me to go to a movie with him tonight," she said. "But I knew I'd be tired from the slumber party, and I was afraid I'd fall asleep on his shoulder in the middle of the movie."

Why did I say that? the real Jana wondered. I'm talking as if I really were Katie.

"What's so terrible about that?" asked the new Jana, laughing softly. "It sounds like fun." Then she glanced at her watch and said, "I can't believe it's six twenty-five already. Randy will be here in five minutes."

"I'd better scoot then," said the real Jana. "Call me in the morning. Okay?"

"Sure," said the new Jana. "Bye."

Jana walked slowly out of the apartment and down the hall trying to understand what had just happened. Why did I act as if I were Katie? And why couldn't I tell her that *I'm* Jana? And who is she, anyway? She has to be one of The Fabulous Five because no one else was at the slumber party, and that's when everything changed. But which one? And if she's one of my best friends, why is she going out with my boyfriend?

As she stepped out the door of the apartment building, she stopped and her eyes widened in horror. Randy Kirwan was coming toward her and he was smiling.

"Hi, Katie," he said, grabbing the door from her. "How's it going?"

Tears choked Jana's throat as she murmured, "Fine," and hurried down the street.

Katie glanced around the Edwardses' kitchen, desperately trying to decide what to say to Melanie's mother. I can't just say, *Guess what? I'm not Melanie*, she thought. There has to be a logical way to explain the situation to her. But what is it?

She twirled a strand of Melanie's reddish-brown hair around a finger and sat down on a stool at the end of the counter and thought about her problem. A plate of Mrs. Edwards's fantastic brownies sat in front of her, and she absently picked up one and began nibbling on it.

I have to convince her that I really am Katie, she decided. That means I have to act like myself. I have to show Melanie's family that I'm a very serious person instead of someone who stares off into space, daydreaming about boys all the time.

Just then Melanie's mother turned away from the sink and glanced toward Katie. She shook her head and said with mild exasperation, "Melanie Edwards. Which boy are you daydreaming about now?"

Katie jerked upright in surprise. Daydreaming? About a boy? What a laugh. Here was her chance to prove to Melanie's mother that she was Katie Shannon and *not* Melanie.

"I was thinking about Shane," Katie was astonished to hear herself say. "He is such a doll, and I haven't really talked to him for a while. I'd love to call him if I could just think of something to say. You know, some important reason to call him at home."

Katie clamped a hand over her mouth. Why on earth had she said that? She had sounded *just like Melanie*. She looked at Mrs. Edwards closely, but Melanie's mother didn't seem the least bit surprised.

"Oh, I'm sure you'll think of something," she said, and then chuckled. "By the way," she added, "Mona Vaughn called last night. She seemed upset that you weren't here and asked me to have you call her as soon as you got home today. In fact, she said it was urgent."

"Oh, no. Not Mona Vaughn," Katie murmured to herself. "She probably wants Melanie to help her cheat again. Well, I'll take care of that!" Furious, Katie headed for the phone to call Mona.

* * *

Melanie had only struggled through half of chapter eighteen in Christie's history book when she slammed the book shut and gazed out the bedroom window. This is the most boring thing I've ever done in my life, she thought. In fact, it's a terrible way to spend a perfectly good Saturday afternoon.

Getting up and pacing around the room, she stared first at the ugly gray history book and then at the beautiful sunny day outside the window. What was she going to do? she wondered. There was no way that she could answer review questions on honors history right now. No way in the world. She needed time, but that wasn't all, she thought, rolling her eyes toward the ceiling. What she really needed was a smarter brain! One that would concentrate on the dull stuff that was in the chapter instead of drifting off to think about Shane Arrington. Or Scott Daly. Or . . .

Her gaze suddenly fell on the neat row of tennis dresses hanging in Christie's closet. She had always thought that wearing the little short skirts and darling tops was the best part of playing the game. Melanie dashed to the closet and pulled out a two-piece outfit made up of a white, pleated skirt trimmed in mauve and a mauve knit top.

"Wow," she said, grinning as she held it up to herself and looked into Christie's full-length mirror. "This is gorgeous." It was still a little bit of a surprise to see Christie's face looking back at her, but most of her attention was on the skirt and top and the impression she would make wearing it. Who on earth would want to sit in a room all alone studying history when she could be dressed like that and having fun?

She didn't even have to look up Jon Smith's phone number. It popped into her head the moment she picked up the receiver. So what if he and Christie weren't dating anymore? She knew he still had a crush on Christie and that they still played tennis together sometimes.

"Hi, Jon," she said brightly when he answered the phone. "What's up?"

"Uh . . . hi!" he said, obviously surprised to hear her voice. "Nothing much. I tried to hit the books, but I'm just not in the mood."

"Me, either," said Melanie. "I was wondering if you'd like to play some tennis." Just then she remembered that Christie had turned down Jon's invitation to the dance and that he might still be upset over that.

"Tennis? You've got to be kidding," said Jon. "I can't believe I'm hearing this after the big lecture you gave me yesterday about having to study all weekend."

Melanie cringed. That certainly sounded like something Christie would do. I'll just have to convince him that I've changed my mind, she thought resolutely.

"Actually, I'm all finished studying," she said in her best Christie voice. "It didn't take as long as I thought it would. Come on. Meet me at the courts in the park in half an hour."

Jon hesitated. "Well . . ." he said, "I guess I could. But only if I bring my math book along and you show me how to work a couple of problems after we finish the set."

"Great," said Melanie. "I'll see you on the courts."

She changed into the mauve and white tennis dress and grabbed Christie's racquet, pausing to admire herself in the mirror again before leaving the room.

She was halfway down the stairs when Mrs. Winchell appeared at the bottom, frowning instantly when she saw Melanie coming down.

"Christie Winchell, where on earth are you going?" she asked angrily. "You know we have to go over the review questions for your history exam. I was just coming up to wake you."

Melanie sat down on the stairs, hugging the racquet and staring at Christie's mother. She let out a long, slow breath while she tried to dream up a suitable excuse.

"Well, young lady," said Mrs. Winchell, "this isn't like you. I'm waiting for an explanation."

"I just needed some fresh air," Melanie began. "My brain was going numb from studying, and I thought a few games of tennis would wake it up, that's all."

Mrs. Winchell put her hands on her hips and looked solemn. "Christie, you know that this is no time to get frivolous about your studying. These exams are critical. Now you march right back up to your room and don't come out until you know that history chapter cold."

Tears jetted into Melanie's eyes, and she wanted to shout, "But I'm not Christie! I'm Melanie, and you can't tell me what to do." But the words wouldn't come out, and there was nothing to do but retreat to Christie's room.

Christie stood just inside Beth's bedroom door, looking down at the silver lamé stretch pants she was wearing and the black sweatshirt with silver lightning bolts across it, and waited for Alicia. She wasn't sure why she had slipped her feet into the shiny silver skimmers she had found on the closet floor instead of the plain black flats sitting next to them, or why she had put on the enormous silver earrings lying on the dresser, but she had.

"Alicia," she called out impatiently. "Where are you? I thought you wanted to come into my room. Besides, I want to talk to you, too." Christie crossed her fingers and prayed silently that Beth's little sister would be able to help her out of the awful predicament she was in.

"In the bathroom," replied a tiny, muffled voice. "I'll be there in a minute."

Christie sat down on Beth's bed and waited. "This had better work," she muttered aloud. "I haven't looked this weird since last Halloween."

She didn't have long to wait because a moment later Alicia came skipping into the room with Agatha bounding along behind her. The huge dog took one look at Christie and loped over to her, woofing loudly and putting her front paws on Christie's shoulders, pushing her backward. The next thing Christie knew, she was lying flat on Beth's bed with Agatha's wet tongue swiping up and down her face.

"Gross!" she muttered under her breath as she tried unsuccessfully to push Agatha away. "Get off of me!" she finally shouted. "Agatha! Get down!"

"What's the matter, Bethy? Don't you love Agafa anymore?" asked Alicia in a pouty voice.

"Of course I love Agatha," Christie said, rolling over on her stomach and covering her head with both arms. At this, Agatha began slurping the back of her neck.

"Good grief! I'm not a snow cone!" she cried, but her words were muffled in the thick comforter covering Beth's bed.

Finally Agatha retreated, settling into a massive lump in the middle of the room and happily thumping her tail against the floor. Sitting up, Christie straightened Beth's gaudy outfit, gingerly picking long dog hairs off it with two fingers, and watching

Agatha out of the corner of her eye in case the shaggy animal decided to come at her again.

That crisis had barely passed when Todd stomped into the room, anger burning in his eyes. "Okay, Alicia, give it back," he demanded.

Alicia folded her arms across her front and glared up at him. "Make me," she challenged.

Todd moved toward Alicia menacingly. "Okay. You asked for it!" Then he grabbed one of her hands and started prying open the fingers one at a time.

At that, Alicia began to howl.

"Hey, you two. What's going on?" yelled Christie, wedging herself between Todd and Alicia and breaking Todd's grip on the little girl's hand.

"I was going to pump up my basketball, and this little monster grabbed the needle and ran," Todd said. His face was getting red and he looked as if he might explode any minute.

Christie threw up her hands in exasperation. "This is dumb," she shouted. "Alicia, what do you have in your hand? Is it the needle to Todd's basketball pump?"

"None of your business," said Alicia, darting back into the hall with Todd right after her.

Agatha perked up her ears and followed, nearly knocking down Brittany, who was scowling as she entered Beth's room.

"Will you three turn down the volume?" she demanded. "I'm trying to talk on the phone!"

Whirling around, she stormed out again, leaving

Christie staring after her in a daze. All I wanted to do was talk to Alicia, and just look what happened, Christie thought. "Oh, my gosh," she whispered in astonishment. "Is this what it's like to be Beth?"

Beth paced the floor of Jana's room as she watched the clock move toward six-thirty and her date with Randy Kirwan. She had never been so nervous in her life. She was glad that Katie had come over for a few minutes. It had helped her to get her mind off the awful fact that she was going out with her best friend's boyfriend. But when the doorbell rang, she nearly jumped through the ceiling.

"Jana, Randy's here," Mrs. Pinkerton called a moment later.

Beth checked the mirror one last time, wishing that Jana had some flashier earrings or a brighter blouse to wear with the jumper. Her heart was thumping as she headed to meet Randy. Would he be able to tell that she wasn't really Jana?

Randy was standing beside the front door talking to Pink and Jana's mother when Beth walked into the living room. His face brightened when he saw her. "Hi, Jana."

Beth returned his greeting, thinking for the millionth time that if she knew, Jana would be absolutely furious at her for spending the entire evening with him. And what about Keith? she wondered in an instant of panic. She had been going with Keith

Masterson since sixth grade. What would *he* think if he ever found out? Would she be able to convince him that she couldn't help it? Would anyone believe that no matter how much she wanted to shout that she was Beth Barry, whenever she opened her mouth she sounded like Jana?

"So, what kind of movie did you get?" she asked after Pink and Mrs. Pinkerton had excused themselves and disappeared.

Randy popped the video cartridge into the VCR and then sat down beside her on the sofa. "A horror flick," he said, laughing devilishly. "It's guaranteed to keep you awake no matter how late you girls talked last night."

All *right*, Beth wanted to say because she loved scary movies. The scarier the better. But instead, her Jana-self looked at him with wide eyes and said, "Oh, Randy, you didn't! You know those things make me jump right out of my skin."

"Don't worry, Jana," he said, giving her a sly wink. "I'm right here!" Then he slid an arm around her and pulled her closer to him.

Beth's eyes widened in alarm. He really did think that she was Jana, and he was starting to get romantic! Where were all of her noisy, meddling brothers and sisters when she needed them? Where was Agatha? And what on earth was she going to do if Randy wanted to kiss her?

CHAPTER

7

*C*hristie closed Beth's bedroom door, hoping to shut out all the confusion. But as she turned and looked around the room, she threw her hands into the air in disgust.

"How can Beth live like this?" she muttered in despair. "It's like being inside a whirling tornado."

Clothes were scattered haphazardly around the floor. The desk was littered with scraps of paper, and a bra hung by its strap from the back of the desk chair. What had once probably been a doughnut was lying, rock hard, in the middle of the unmade bed. Christie had never seen so much clutter in her life. But the worst, the *very* worst to Christie's way of thinking, were the walls, which Beth had painted white, then decorated with pieces of brightly colored adhesive tape. One wall was covered with slashes of green horizontal stripes. Vertical yellow marks rained down the wall next to that. Then came electric-blue diagonal lines on the third wall, slanting toward bright-red zigzags that danced crazily on the fourth. "How in the world does she sleep?" Christie whispered in amazement.

Sighing deeply, she realized that if she was going to have to inhabit Beth's body for the time being, that meant she was going to have to live in Beth's room, too. She thought fleetingly of her own immaculate room, neat almost to the point of perfection, and then started cleaning up Beth's massive mess like a whirlwind. Clothes went into a pile in the corner, to be sorted and laundered later. The doughnut was plucked with two fingers and dropped with a thud into the unused wastebasket. She made the bed and then settled down to the monumental task of straightening up Beth's desk.

"Look at this! What a disaster," Christie complained aloud. "It's no wonder she has trouble studying. Once I get this mess organized, she'll be a lot better off."

The top of the desk was covered with scraps of paper, old notes, outdated school assignments, names, phone numbers, and assorted odds and ends. *Garbage*, all of it, Christie decided as she raised one hand and swiped it all into the wastebasket.

Next she dug Beth's math book out from under her bed, located her other books in various parts of the room, and lined them up in a neat row on the desk.

"There," she said, sitting back and looking around with satisfaction. "Now maybe she'll be able to accomplish something. Or I will, as long as I *have* to be Beth."

"Hey, Beth. You've got a phone call."

Brian's voice startled her. She hadn't even heard the phone ring. "Coming," she called out to him, and hurried to take the call.

"Hi, Beth. It's Whitney Larkin. I can't find the list of kids on my ticket sales committee and I need to talk to them. I must have accidentally thrown it away. Would you give it to me again?"

"The list of kids on your committee," Christie stated flatly as she tried to comprehend what Whitney was asking. "Oh! The kids on your committee!" She understood now. Beth was on all the dance committees and was in charge of pulling some of them together. But where would she have put the lists of names?

"Whitney, can I call you back?" Christie asked quickly. "I have to find my notes."

She raced back to Beth's room certain that she knew where the notes were. She stopped cold just inside the door, staring at the spot where the wastebasket had been just moments ago. "What's going on here?" she moaned. "Somebody stole the trash."

She was heading back into the hall to track down

the missing wastebasket when the phone rang again. "Hello," she said in a breathless voice. "Barry residence."

"Oh, Beth. I'm glad you're home." It was Mandy McDermott and she sounded panicky. "Listen, I hate to do this, but I'm going to have to drop off the dance committee. You'll have to get someone else to buy the paper cups and stuff. My parents threw a fit when they saw my grade on the last math test and said I can't do anything that's extracurricular until after exams."

"But, Mandy . . ." Christie started to protest. At the same time she saw Brian sauntering along the upstairs hall carrying three wastebasekts, all empty. Oh, my gosh, she thought. It's Saturday, probably housecleaning day at the Barrys', and it's Brian's job to empty the wastebaskets.

"Sorry. My lords and masters have spoken," Mandy was saying. "I must obey."

"Sure," Christie mumbled. "I'll get somebody else. Thanks for calling."

She smashed the receiver down and went streaking toward the garage. She had seen trash cans there before, and she had to go through them and get the stuff she had swept off Beth's desk before it was too late.

Three trash cans sat in the corner. Christie pulled the lid off the first one and peered inside. Empty. The second was empty, too, but when she opened the third one, she almost dropped the lid. It was three-quarters full, and there were definitely scraps of paper with Beth's handwriting on them in it, but to her absolute horror the whole thing was covered with a reeking pile of orange peels, cottage cheese, and spaghetti complete with meatballs and sauce.

"Oh, *yuck*!" she shrieked, slamming the lid down again. She sank against the garage wall and tried to think. She really needed those notes. Otherwise what was she going to do about the dance committees? Maybe, if she was really careful, she could pick around in the garbage and find the notes without touching anything gross.

Slowly and cautiously she pulled off the lid as if a putrid meatball were lurking inside waiting to reach out and grab her. Of course it didn't, but the sight of the awful mess made her stomach roll.

Christie reached forward, using her fingers like pincers, and tugged at an unsoiled piece of paper. She carefully steered it around a splot of spaghetti sauce as she extracted it, snagging a long string of spaghetti on the way up. Mercifully, the spaghetti dropped off. Christie sighed with relief. Unfolding the paper, she groaned as she saw that it was only Beth's class assignments from three weeks ago.

She stared into the trash can again. She couldn't. She just couldn't stir around in that mess, no matter what. She'd just have to think of another way to get the information she needed on the committees. She sighed as she trudged back up the stairs. So much for getting Beth's life organized.

* * *

Jana hurried back toward Katie's house, trying to push thoughts of Randy and the fake Jana out of her mind. For now she had to concentrate on the fact that she was in Katie's body and try to figure out a way to get out. Only then would she be able to deal with Randy and the imposter who was with him right now.

Jana also knew that Katie had her own problems. Take Tony, for instance, and what Funny had told Jana about Tony's spending a lot of time at Shawnie Pendergast's house lately. Jana had really been surprised when Katie said she wasn't going to confront Tony about it unless she got more proof.

The least she could do is ask him about it, thought Jana. I'd do that if it were Randy.

It was almost dark now, and Jana quickened her step, knowing that she should hurry home before Willie checked her bedroom and found her gone. Looking around in surprise, Jana found that she was walking down Shawnie's street. Why did I come this way? she wondered. It was definitely the long way home.

Shawnie's parents both had big careers and their house was on one of the most expensive streets in town. Jana stopped two houses away and looked wistfully at the gorgeous yard and neat flower beds, things she had never had because she had lived in apartments ever since she could remember. Just then she spotted a bicycle on the front sidewalk. It was hard to see at first in the gathering dusk, but it was Tony's bicycle, and it was parked in the same spot where she had seen it a few days ago.

As she stood there, the front door opened and Tony walked out with Shawnie following him closely. They were talking, and Jana thought she could hear Shawnie's tinkling laugh.

"Poor Katie!" she said, louder than she had meant to. But neither Tony nor Shawnie had seen her standing in the shadows. The next instant Tony hopped on his bike and pedaled away.

Jana waited until Shawnie had gone back inside, then she scuffed angrily toward the Shannon house. "Look out, Tony Calcaterra," she muttered as she walked along. "The real Katie might let you get away with this, but I won't!"

Beth sat stiff as a poker with Randy's arm draped casually around her shoulder, trying not to panic. Each time the ghoul in the movie crept out from behind a bush or faded into the shadows, Randy would give her a little squeeze. Then he would lean toward her and whisper, "Don't worry, Jana. I'm right here. I'll protect you."

The trouble was, each time he leaned toward her, he also scooted a little closer. A couple more scenes with the ghoul and she would practically be in his lap.

"Why don't I make some popcorn?" she said brightly, launching herself off the sofa and into the direction of the kitchen. It was the perfect solution. She could set the bowl between them. That way he wouldn't be able to kiss her.

When she looked around, Randy was giving her a puzzled look. "We don't need any popcorn *now*," he grumbled, following her into the kitchen.

"Of course we do," Beth insisted. "And some sodas. I'd better check the ice-cube trays. Sometimes Mom forgets to fill them." She knew she was rambling, but she had to do something. And having sodas *and* popcorn was an even better idea. He'd have to hold the soda in one hand and eat popcorn with the other.

She pulled two glasses out of the cupboard and dashed to the refrigerator. Grabbing an ice-cube tray, she tried to twist out the cubes, but her hands were shaking so badly that she sent the ice flying all over the room.

"Whoops!" she said, and flashed Randy an embarrassed grin as she stooped to the floor and scrambled around, retrieving the rapidly melting ice cubes and pitching them over her head into the sink.

Randy shook his head. It was obvious that he was annoyed. "Come on, Jana. We don't need any refreshments right now. Come on back and watch the movie."

"Sure we do," she said. "I'm thirsty. Aren't you

thirsty? And hungry. I'll make us a bi-i-g bowl of hot, buttery popcorn. Okay?"

Randy shrugged and poured some Coke into his glass. Then he went back into the living room, leaving her standing alone beside the counter.

Beth bit her lower lip and sighed. Randy was angry. There was no question about it. But what else could she do? She certainly couldn't let him kiss her. Not Randy, her best friend's boyfriend!

Popcorn, she thought. Oh, my gosh. I don't know where Jana's mother keeps it. Beth began banging cupboard doors, frantically searching for the popcorn. Jana made it lots of times when The Fabulous Five came over. Why couldn't she remember where it was kept?

Maybe I could whip out something else, thought Beth. Cookies. All guys like cookies. But she couldn't find any cookies either. She was looking dejectedly around the kitchen when she heard the front door slam. Beth frowned. Had someone just come in?

Then a terrible thought occurred to her. "Randy?" she called. Dashing into the living room, she saw the movie still playing on the television with the ghoul creeping silently across a moonlight-drenched landscape. She also saw Randy's half-empty soda glass sitting on the table. But no Randy.

She rushed to the window just in time to see him striding across the street and out of sight.

"On, no," she whispered. "What have I done?"

* * *

Katie was sure that Mona Vaughn must have been sitting beside the phone, because she answered before it had finished its first ring.

"Oh, Melanie. I'm so glad you called," she gushed as soon as Katie said hello. "Those answers you gave me for the history test saved my life. I mean, *really* . . . *saved* . . . *my* . . . *life*!"

Sirens started going off in Katie's brain. She had been right. Melanie had given Mona the answers to the history exam, just as she had suspected. How could Melanie have done such a thing? She had to know it was wrong.

"Mr. Naset called me up to his desk after class this afternoon to show me my grade," Mona went on before Katie could respond. "He gave me a B, an actual B! Isn't that fantastic? Now I won't flunk the course. And Melanie, if you hadn't given me those answers, I would definitely have flunked. You're a wonderful friend. Thank you! Thank you! *Thank* you!"

Katie crossed her eyes in frustration. Now what was she going to do? How was she going to handle this? Mona thought she was talking to the real Melanie, and the real Melanie had helped her cheat. Well, one thing is certain, Katie thought resolutely, I can't let them get away with it. Not either of them.

"I need to talk to you, Mona, face-to-face and in

private," said Katie. "It's really important. Can you come over now?"

"Gosh, no," said Mona. "My grandma is coming for the weekend and she'll be here any minute. I'm stuck here until school on Monday."

Katie sighed impatiently. "Okay," she conceded. "I guess it can wait until Monday, but promise me you'll meet me by the front gate before school."

"Okay," Mona agreed, but Katie could hear apprehension in her voice. "If you say so. See you then. Bye."

Melanie may not appreciate it, Katie thought after she hung up, but I'm doing her a humongous favor by getting her out of trouble before she gets in any deeper.

When Melanie entered Christie's room again, the big, gray history book lay open on the desk. "It looks like a toad!" Melanie spat out the words. "A fat, ugly toad! And I don't want to touch it, much less study all that boring history."

She spun around so that her back was to the book and crossed her arms over her chest, as if ignoring it would make it go away. The next instant her anger gave way to self-pity. "What I really want to do is play tennis with Jon," she whispered.

"Oh, my gosh! Jon!" Melanie raced to the desk and grabbed the receiver, stabbing at the key pad as she punched in his number. "Oh, please answer. Please."

As the slow, steady ring sounded in her ear, Melanie tried to imagine why it was taking Jon so long to answer. Maybe he was still in his room, changing into his tennis shorts with his stereo going full blast and couldn't hear the phone. Or in the bathroom. Or maybe he had just taken a big bite of a sandwich and had to chew and swallow it before he could talk. That happened to her all the time.

Oh, please answer, she said silently to herself. Be there. I'll die if you've already left for the park because then you'll think I'm standing you up.

But the phone rang on and on.

If only someone was home to take a message, she thought. But she knew that Jon's parents were seldom home. They were both local television personalities, and when they weren't at the station doing shows, they were out taping interviews and things like that.

Finally, after about the zillionth ring, Melanie replaced the receiver. Jon was going to be angry, and so would the real Christie, if she knew about it. But I tried, Melanie thought in her own defense. I really did try.

Taking a deep breath, she faced the awful history book. She had the feeling that she had really messed up things between Christie and Jon. And now, thanks to Mrs. Winchell, she had no choice but to study for a test in honors history. How on earth was she going to keep from messing that up, too?

CHAPTER

8

A little tremor went through Beth in anticipation of seeing her friends as she approached the Wakeman Junior High school grounds on Monday morning. She had called Christie, Katie, and Melanie over the weekend, but no matter how hard she had tried, somehow she couldn't tell them she was Beth in Jana's body. She was afraid to call her own home to see if another Beth answered, and now as she entered the school grounds, she wondered if there would be a Beth standing by the fence. Would she be able to identify who it was?

As she walked through the school gates, she saw Christie, Katie, Melanie, and sure enough, someone who looked exactly the way she did when she was Beth standing at The Fabulous Five's spot by the fence. She pulled back her shoulders and walked over to them.

"Hi, Jana," Katie said, giving her a big smile. The others turned and said hello, too. Beth searched their faces to try to detect whether any of them saw anything strange about her. If they did, they didn't show it.

As the others returned to the conversation they had been having about the dance, Beth very carefully looked over the imposter who looked like her real self. She *had* to be in Beth's body because Beth couldn't see anything about her that was different or didn't belong. There were no freckles or moles or anything like that. Her hair was brushed down instead of sticking up in the spiky way she liked to wear it, but that was the only thing that wasn't quite right. A little feeling of pride went through Beth. Her body *was* pretty cute, even when she wasn't in it.

"Have you seen her, Jana?" asked Melanie.

The question startled Beth. She hadn't been listening and had forgotten for a moment she was in Jana's body. "Er . . . seen who?"

"Mona. I need to talk to her."

"No, I haven't," Beth said, looking around the schoolyard. Randy was just parking his bike at the bike rack. "Maybe Mona's gone to her locker."

"I think I'll go check," said Melanie. "It's important." She headed for the front door.

Beth watched Randy to see if he would look for her in her Jana body. Jana always talked about what a sincere and understanding person Randy was. Would he still be mad about Saturday night?

Katie found Mona kneeling on the floor and rummaging through things in the bottom of her locker.

"Oh, hi, Melanie," Mona said brightly.

Being called Melanie was still a shock to Katie.

"I'm looking for some bubble mix. I just know I had an extra bottle in here somewhere." Mona went to the humane society after school a couple of times a week to visit the animals. She used the bubble mix to blow bubbles for the dogs and cats to play with. Katie knew Mona had a heart of gold, and it was making it even tougher for her to be angry at her for getting Melanie to do a dumb thing such as giving her the answers to the history test. "Mona, I need to talk to you," said Katie. "It's about the history test."

Mona looked up at Katie from where she was kneeling, and a bright smile burst across her normally plain face. "Oh, yes. I want to thank you again and again for helping me, Melanie. You *really* are a supernice person, you know. *Everyone* says you're the nicest person in all of Wacko. If I can ever do anything for you, you know all you have to do is ask."

"That's okay," said Katie, confused. How did you chew out someone while they were telling you how fantastic you were? Just as she was bracing herself for another try, Dekeisha Adams came up.

"Oh, Melanie, am I glad to see you," the tall black girl said. "I need your advice. Can we talk where it's private?"

"Uh, sure, I was . . ."

"Don't mind me," said Mona, scrambling to her feet. "I found my bubble mix, and I've got to get to class. See you two later," she said, hurrying off.

Dekeisha looked both ways to see if anyone was listening and then spoke in a guarded voice. "No one knows this, Melanie, and you've got to promise not to tell. Swear?" Katie nodded. "Good. This is my problem," Dekeisha continued, excitement building in her voice. "I really want the new guy, Don Petry, to ask me to the dance, but I can't get him to pay any attention to me. Since you're kind of an expert on boys," she said, touching Katie's arm, "I wondered if you could give me some advice on what to do. I'll be in your debt forever," she added with a pleading look in her eyes.

Katie knew Don Petry. His family had just recently moved to town. He was good-looking and very tall, and since Dekeisha was tall, too, they would make a super-looking couple. Katie tried to think of how to respond. While it was true that Melanie knew a lot about boys—she should since she studied them more than she did her school work—Katie didn't. She had dated only one boy in her life, Tony, and that certainly didn't qualify her as an expert. "Uh, have you tried talking to him?" she asked.

Dekeisha looked slightly annoyed at the suggestion. "Of course I've tried talking to him. He just kind of grunts back and ignores me." She looked expectantly at Katie, waiting for her to come up with a better idea.

Katie tried desperately to remember Melanie's seven flirting tips. What were they? If only she had listened to Melanie recite them for once instead of jumping all over her for being so boy crazy. As Katie stared back at Dekeisha, one of the tips suddenly popped into her mind. "Do you look Don in the eyes?" she asked quickly.

Dekeisha gave a sigh of frustration. "Where else would I look at him? In the nose?"

"Well, no, of course not," said Katie. "But it's one of the *first* and *most important* things to do. Look," she said, trying to buy some time to look through Melanie's notebook, where she was sure she would find the flirting tips written down. "The bell's about to ring. Why don't I write some flirting tips down and give them to you at lunch?"

"That would be fantastic," said Dekeisha. "But don't forget them. My life depends on it."

Why were all these things happening to her? Katie asked herself. Now, besides getting Melanie out of trouble for helping Mona on the history test, she had to advise Dekeisha on how to get Don Petry to ask her to the dance. All this, on top of having to figure out how to get out of Melanie's body and back into her own. She gave a big sigh and trudged off to Melanie's next class.

Melanie had been glad to get out of Christie's house on Monday morning and out from under the watchful eye of Mrs. Winchell. Christie's mother had hounded her all weekend about the honors history test. At the same time, she had been in a panic. What was it going to be like being Christie Winchell at Wacko Junior High?

First, there was the problem of facing Jon. Melanie had finally reached him by phone on Sunday afternoon, concocting a teensy little lie about coming down the stairs too fast and twisting her ankle just as she was leaving to meet him at the park. Actually the lie had grown from teensy to medium size to huge once he had been so totally concerned and sympathetic that he had forgiven her for standing him up, and she had let the twist grow into a full-fledged sprain. She knew she would have to remember to limp, and she had come up with a brilliant idea to help her with that little problem. She had stuck a piece of gravel from her driveway down into her left shoe, and each time she tried to step down on it, the pain forced her to limp.

But what could help her with the honors history

test? Melanie's mouth turned dry and her palms sweaty every time she thought about it. Taking a deep breath, she entered the classroom and sank slowly into Christie's seat behind Curtis Trowbridge.

Curtis spun around. "Hi, Chris," he said, and smiled confidently. "Test's going to be a snap. Right?"

Melanie nodded mutely. A snap? You've *got* to be kidding, she thought. Not only did Miss Jamal, who was from somewhere in the Middle East, look old enough to have lived through most of the history in their textbook, but she had the reputation of giving killer tests. Even brains like Christie complained about her.

"How can I *possibly* pass this test?" she whimpered softly once Curtis had turned back around in his seat.

Miss Jamal shuffled slowly into the room, her face set into a concrete frown. She plunked her ancient leather briefcase onto her desk without looking at the class and extracted a handful of papers.

Test papers. Melanie shuddered. This was it. The moment of truth. Miss Jamal was going to be the first person in the universe to discover she wasn't really Christie. But no! she reasoned, frowning. Miss Jamal will think I really am Christie and that I'm brain dead. She'll flunk Christie flat. And then when the real Christie finds out, I'll be the one who's dead, and it will be more than just my brain.

Melanie scrunched down, trying to make herself as small as possible, and covered her face with her hands.

"Beth Barry, I waited all weekend for you to call me back and tell me who is on my committee."

Whitney Larkin raced up to Christie at the top of the stairs, and like everyone else, she was sure that Christie was Beth.

"Gosh, Whitney. I'm really sorry," Christie said. "I . . . I . . ." she fumbled. What excuse could she possibly make?

"Listen, I don't have time to talk right now," said Whitney. "I have to meet Curtis, but I'll catch you in the cafeteria at noon. Okay?"

"Sure," said Christie. She watched Whitney dodge through the crowd with a feeling of relief. At least she had bought a little more time. But what good would that do? How was she going to find out who was on that committee without making a complete idiot of herself? Or of Beth? she reminded herself.

It wasn't as if she hadn't tried. She had spent the weekend doing everything short of digging through the garbage again to try to find Beth's dance committee notes and identify the members of all the committees Beth was on. She had searched Beth's school notebook page by page only to find it a total jumble of class assignments and doodles, with nothing, not a single mention, of the dance committees or their members. Next she had tried the logical approach. Who would Beth ask to be on her committees? But the only logical answer she came up with was The Fabulous Five, and she knew for certain that none of them had volunteered. That left her back at square one and with a deadline of noon in the cafeteria to come up with the answer.

As she looked around in frustration, she saw Keith Masterson coming toward her. "Why the long face?" he asked, giving her a playful nudge.

Christie could feel herself blushing ever so slightly. It was hard to remember that Keith thought she was Beth, and it felt strange to see her friend's boyfriend looking at her so affectionately.

"Oh, you know how disorganized I am," she said, letting out an exasperated sigh. "I've lost my dance committee notes, and I know it's weird, but I can't for the life of me remember who's on any of my committees."

Keith let his arms droop and he gave her a dumb-founded look. "Thanks a lot," he muttered sar-castically. "It's nice to know that our relationship is so important to you."

Christie swallowed hard. Uh-oh, she thought. I bet I've blown it now.

"What do you mean?" she asked in a tiny voice.

Keith narrowed his eyes and frowned at her, look-ing as if he couldn't believe what she had just said. "Oh, so you really don't remember that I'm on every single committee with you, huh? Then don't be surprised if *I* forget that I asked you to the dance."

Before Christie could even begin to think of a way to answer him, someone in the crowd bumped against her, causing her to do a juggling act to keep her books from plummeting to the floor. When she looked up, Keith was gone.

I've got to find him, she thought desperately. I've simply got to find a way to tell him that I'm not Beth. I've got to explain what's happened and ask for his help. But how can I explain, she wondered, when I don't even understand it myself?

Jana had been on the lookout for Tony Calcaterra ever since she came inside the school building. She had spotted Shawnie Pendergast talking to Taffy Sinclair on the front sidewalk, so at least Tony wasn't spending time with her at school. But she was dying to see how he would act toward Katie now that he was sneaking around and going to see Shawnie on the sly.

"That rat!" Jana muttered between clenched teeth. It made her all the more furious at him to know that even though he hadn't actually asked Katie to the dance, Katie was sure they would be going together. She was even shopping for a special dress. It would be a disaster if he took Shawnie instead.

"Yo there, Your Honor."

Jana jumped at the sound of Tony's voice. That

was his standard greeting for Katie, and Jana had heard him say it a thousand times, but it was a weird sensation to hear him saying it to her.

Jana straightened her shoulders and raised her chin as she faced him. "Hi," she said icily. Then she turned and strode purposefully in the direction of Katie's locker.

"Hey, beautiful. Hey, you with the gorgeous red hair. Wait up," he called as he hurried after her.

Grrrr, thought Jana. Just listen to him. He has a guilty conscience so he's trying to win Katie over with flattery. Randy Kirwan would never do a thing like that. Randy's sincere. In fact, he's the kindest and most sincere boy in the entire world. Tony Calcaterra is a jerk!

She sailed on down the hall with her nose in the air, leaving him far behind. She would show him a thing or two and save Katie's dignity at the same time.

CHAPTER

9

*M*elanie looked down at the test paper in front of her and automatically wrote her name in the top right-hand corner: Christie Winchell. Little beads of perspiration popped out on her forehead as she read down the questions. They were all about England in the 1500s, and although she had read the chapters carefully, or had tried to, the names and dates in the questions sounded only vaguely familiar.

She looked around at the other students, who sat hunched over their tests, their pencils flying across the pages. Curtis Trowbridge, Whitney Larkin, Melissa McConnell, and all the rest of the brainy seventh-graders who were enrolled in honors history. Her heart sank. They looked so confident. So *prepared*. Why hadn't she studied harder? she wondered. Read the chapters more carefully? Taken notes?

"I still wouldn't be able to pass an honors history test," she grumbled under her breath.

"Did you have a question, Christie?" Miss Jamal asked in her slightly accented voice.

"No, ma'am," Melanie replied, looking quickly at her paper.

She put in a few answers about King Henry VIII that she actually knew. He had been fun to read about, although she had had a hard time imagining how anyone could have six wives and murder three of them just because he got mad at them. But the answers to the other questions on the test were a mystery to her, and the minutes dragged by endlessly until the dismissal bell rang.

"I blew it," she muttered as she limped into the hall on the painful piece of gravel. "I studied all weekend on that rotten stuff, and I just flunked Christie's test for her. Now what am I going to do?"

Melanie glanced around the busy hallway as if she expected to get a clue to her dilemma written somewhere on the walls. Instead, her gaze fell on Jon, who was coming toward her with an odd look on his face.

"I don't get it, Christie," he said when he stopped before her.

"Don't get what?" Melanie asked.

"Your limp," he said. "I saw you just now."

Melanie let out an exasperated sigh. "I told you what happened. I twisted my ankle coming down the stairs when I was leaving to meet you for our tennis game. That's why I never showed up. I thought you understood that."

"I do. I do," Jon assured her. "It's just that you said on the phone that you twisted your right ankle. So if that's true, how come you're limping on your left foot?"

Melanie cringed. Did I say right foot or left foot? she asked herself, but she honestly couldn't remember.

"Maybe I said right foot when I meant left," she offered weakly. She knew it was a lame excuse, but it was all she could think of on the spur of the moment.

Jon backed off a couple of steps, shaking his head and looking at her as if he couldn't believe what he was seeing. "I don't know about you, Christie," he said in a flat voice. "You haven't been acting like yourself for the past few days. I'm not sure what's happening, but I'll tell you one thing. I liked the old Christie better."

With that, he whirled around and left her standing in the middle of the hall.

For the first time since Christie had wakened on Saturday morning in Beth's body, she felt as if she might be about to get things under control. She was glad that she had thought of the idea of talking to Keith. She knew how much he cared for Beth, in spite of how angry he was right now. Surely he would be able to help her find some way to bring all this craziness to an end if she could just figure out how to explain what was going on.

She was still thinking about this as she pushed her tray along the hot-lunch line when she heard someone behind her call Beth's name.

"Oh, hi, Kaci," she said, looking back to see Kaci Davis smiling in her direction.

"Beth, don't forget that the committee meets in the media center after school to plan how many paper cups, napkins, and that sort of stuff to buy for the dance."

"Oh, wow. Thanks for reminding me," Christie said. Then her brain kicked into high gear. "You don't happen to remember who's on that committee, do you? I can't find my list anywhere."

Kaci gave her a miffed look. "Of course I do. I'm chairman of the *entire* dance, you know. I have a list of *all* the committees."

Christie tried her best to imitate Beth's disorganized manner. Smiling apologetically, she said, "Gosh, can I copy them down? I'd really appreciate it. You know how much trouble I have keeping track of things."

Kaci grumbled something that Christie couldn't hear. Then in a little louder voice she said, "Okay," and whipped a sheet of paper out of her notebook, handing it to Christie. "But don't forget to give it back to me before you leave the cafeteria."

"You bet," Christie assured her.

"And don't spill anything on it either," Kaci cautioned over her shoulder as she whirled around to join her friends.

Christie had to chuckle at that remark. Even Kaci Davis, who was a ninth-grader, realized how off the wall Beth could be sometimes. She copied the lists and was amazed to find that Keith had been telling the truth. Not only was Beth on every single committee, but so was he. He had obviously joined them to be with her. No wonder he was so steamed when I didn't know that, she thought. She returned the paper to Kaci and stopped by Whitney's lunch table to tell her who else was on her committee and then looked around for Keith. Unfortunately, he was nowhere to be seen. He's probably ducking me because he's so mad, she decided.

She didn't see him in the halls between Beth's afternoon classes either, and when she entered the media center after school, she thought at first that he wasn't going to show up for the committee meeting. Then she spotted him at one of the far tables, his nose stuck in a magazine.

Acting as casual as she could, Christie sauntered over to him and sat down. "Hi," she said shyly.

"Hi, Beth," he answered without looking up.

"I'm sorry about what I said earlier . . . you

know, about not knowing who was on my committees. But if anybody knows how scatterbrained I
am, it's you. And I *definitely* remembered that you
were on the committees, no matter how it sounded."

Keith chewed his lower lip and pretended to study
the sports car advertisement on the magazine page.
Christie knew he was thinking over what she had
just said, and she kept her fingers crossed that she
had said it right and that he would believe her.

Finally he sighed and looked up at her. "You really
keep me guessing sometimes. I mean, I never know
what crazy thing you're going to say next."

"Right," Christie said slowly. Just wait, she
thought. You ain't heard nothing yet!

"Okay," he said, his face lighting up with a smile.
"I believe you. Besides, I don't really want to be
mad."

Christie breathed a big sigh of relief. Now, if she
could just get the rest of the conversation to go the
way she had planned.

"There's something else," she said, and he looked
at her questioningly. "Something I need to say."

Keith moved his chair closer to hers. It made her
feel instantly better, and she rehearsed for the hundredth time that day what she wanted to say.

*Keith, I know this will sound strange, but I'm really
Christie.* She shot a quick look at him. He was gazing
at her, waiting for her to speak and looking as if he
expected it to be something totally normal.

Keith, I know this will sound strange, but I'm really

Christie, she began again in her mind. *When I went to sleep Friday night at Katie's slumber party, I was myself. But when I woke up, I was in Beth's body. I need your help getting back to my real self and helping Beth become Beth again. Okay?*

"Come on, Beth. What was it you wanted to tell me?" Keith urged.

Christie squared her shoulders. She had to say it. Just the way she had rehearsed. She opened her mouth and tried to say, *Keith, I know this will sound strange.* But the words that came out instead amazed her.

"I just wanted to say that I hoped you didn't mean it when you said you might not take me to the dance."

"Oh, is that all?" asked Keith. He looked relieved. "Of course I'm taking you to the dance."

"There's something else," she added quickly.

"Sure," he said. "Fire."

This time she rested her chin on her open hand, determined to help her lips move correctly if she had to. She swallowed hard and thought about the words again. *Keith, I know this will sound strange.* Okay, she thought. I'm ready. "I'm just glad that you aren't really mad," Beth's voice assured him.

Across the room Kaci was calling the committee members to the meeting. A wad of panic filled Christie's throat. Why couldn't she say the words she had planned? Why couldn't she tell him who she really was?

"Hey, you know how I feel about you," Keith said, giving her arm a playful punch. "Come on, we'd better join the others for the meeting."

Beth sat in study hall and doodled in Jana's notebook. She had decided that since Randy was so honest and sincere, the best way to straighten things out with him was the direct approach. That's what Jana would do. She would stand at the intersection of the two hallways where she knew Jana always waited for Randy so they could walk to their next class together. Then she would apologize for the way she had acted Saturday night and everything would be okay between him and Jana again.

If she *didn't* make up with Randy, the real Jana would kill her if she ever got her body back. Beth changed that to *when* Jana got her body back. Where could the real Jana be right now? she wondered. She obviously wasn't in this body or Beth would know it. Would they be able to talk to each other? In spite of herself, Beth giggled at the thought of being crowded into the same body with Jana. *Was* Jana the person in Beth's body? If that was true, she hoped Jana was taking good care of it.

Beth had her books closed and stacked when the bell rang and she was the first one out of the room. She didn't want to take a chance on missing Randy. He might think that she was avoiding him.

"Ooops! Sorry," she said as she bumped into

someone and dropped two of her books. As she reached down to pick them up, Keith Masterson, the boy she had been going with since the sixth grade, bent to help her. She nearly melted down into her shoes when she realized it was him, and he smiled at her.

"That's okay, Jana," Keith said. "I wasn't watching where I was going. Here, let me get those."

As he handed the books to her, their hands touched, and Beth felt a tingle ripple through her arms and into her body.

Without thinking she did the most natural thing for her, which was to slip her arm through Keith's. As they walked together, she impulsively started chattering to him about the school dance. He laughed at what she was saying, and she put her head against his shoulder. As they turned a corner, they nearly ran into Randy Kirwan. Randy's face froze in disbelief at the sight of her, in Jana's body, and Keith locked arm in arm. Beth had a sinking feeling in the pit of her stomach as Randy turned on his heel and disappeared into the crowd. How in the world was she going to explain this to Randy?

Katie leafed through Melanie's notebook looking for her list of flirting tips for Dekeisha. She was sure they had to be in there. Melanie would never leave home without them. Finally she found the list on a page with Scott Daly's, Shane Arrington's, and Garrett Boldt's names scribbled all around the border along with drawings of little hearts with arrows through them. Katie shook her head in amazement. Didn't Melanie ever think of anything besides boys and romance? Well, at least she had found the tips and could write them down and give them to De-keisha, who was sitting two rows over, when the final bell rang. She read down the list.

1. *Make eye contact with the boy you are flirt-ing with.*

There were little eyeballs drawn all around number one.

2. *Act happy and self-confident.*

This time the drawings were of all kinds of smil-ing mouths.

3. *Use positive body language.*
4. *Give compliments.*
5. *Show genuine interest in him.*
6. *Ask him questions.*
7. *Be a good listener.*

They were all common sense, once you thought about it. She didn't think they would impress De-keisha as being especially original, either. Katie thought and thought. What would be better? For one thing, she and Tony were very honest and straightforward with each other. That was what she liked about him, and he had said it was what he liked about her. It was really the only way for a boy and girl to be. None of this grinning at each other, blinking eyes, and acting interested in what the other person was saying, whether you were or not. That way you *knew* where you stood and didn't imagine things that weren't true.

That's it! she said to herself. She tore a blank page out of the notebook and wrote:

> *Whatever you do, tell him exactly what you think. Boys like girls who are honest with them. If he's wearing a dumb-loking shirt, tell him so. Also, make sure he treats you like an equal. He'll respect you for it.*

Katie read over what she had written. Yes, that was much better, she thought.

The bell rang as Katie was folding the paper. She caught up with Dekeisha at the door and gave it to her. "Here," she said with a smile. "I hope this helps. It certainly worked for me."

Dekeisha gave her a big grin. "Oh, thanks, Mel. I'll invite you to our wedding in ten years."

Katie felt good about what she had done. Melanie couldn't have given Dekeisha any better advice.

* * *

Jana smiled to herself as she walked to Bumpers. The look on Tony Calcaterra's face when she sailed past him in the hall in Katie's body was worth seeing. *Now* maybe he would be sorry that he was cheating on Katie. She was glad Randy wasn't like Tony. But who was that girl who was wearing her denim outfit and had a date with Randy? Jana knew Randy would be *really* mad when he found out it wasn't the real her.

There was one good thing about being in someone else's body. She didn't have to think about what to get her two fathers for Father's Day for a while. But the bad thing was she couldn't be with her mother either. Somehow the little bathroom crammed with all of Pink's things and the living room overflowing with his bowling trophies didn't seem so bad anymore. She dug a tissue out of her purse and blew her nose.

When Jana entered Bumpers, she saw Melanie, Christie, and the fake Jana sitting in a booth in the corner. "Hi, Katie," called Christie, waving to get her attention. Jana walked over and slid into the booth next to her.

For some reason, Melanie seemed to be staring at her. Could Melanie tell that she wasn't really Katie? Jana eagerly opened her mouth to tell Melanie that she was really Jana, but all that came out was, "Hi, Melanie. How's Rainbow?"

Melanie gave Jana a quizzical look. "She's fine. Thanks for asking."

Jana could feel her face turning red. Why had she just asked Melanie about her dog? No matter how hard she tried, she didn't seem able to tell anyone that she was really Jana, trapped in Katie's body. "Where's Beth?" she asked quickly, trying to cover up her embarrassment.

"She's staying after school for another one of her dance committee meetings," said Christie.

Jana got up to get a soda and looked around Bumpers to see who else was there. Two people were obviously missing—Tony and Shawnie. Heat worked its way up Jana's collar. It looked as if Tony hadn't learned a lesson after all. The next step is to save Katie's pride and break up with him completely, thought Jana. Once things are back to normal, Katie will appreciate it.

CHAPTER

10

*J*ana strolled along in deep thought as she headed for Katie's house after leaving Bumpers. If she was going to break up with Tony for Katie's sake, she had to do it in a way that would *totally* convince Katie that she had done the right thing. In addition, there had to be proof that Tony was cheating on Katie. Like a flash of lightning, a colossal idea hit her. Jana grinned to herself and turned at the next corner and headed away from Katie's house.

As she approached Shawnie's house, Jana stepped behind a big tree that kept her out of view from the Pendergasts'. She craned her neck to look over the brick wall that surrounded the big house. Tony's bike was parked by the front steps again. Jana shook her head in disgust. He was spending nearly all of his spare time with Shawnie.

Jana checked her watch. It was getting close to dinnertime, and unless he was going to eat with the Pendergasts, Tony ought to be coming out pretty soon. Jana dashed across the street and hid behind the wall. From there she could see the whole house. It was impressive with its big rolling lawn and three stories. She bet herself that there was a swimming pool in back. Putting her books down on the sidewalk, Jana sat on them to wait.

Five minutes later the front door opened, and Tony and Shawnie came out onto the front porch. They chatted for a few minutes and then Jana heard Tony say, "I'll see you tomorrow." Jana leapt to her feet and marched up to the porch steps with her fists on her hips. Tony stopped in his tracks, his eyes opened wide in surprise.

"Katie?" said Shawnie. "What are *you* doing here?"

"*It should be obvious why I'm here*," said Jana in her iciest voice. Then, glaring at Tony, she said, "What *I'd* like to know is what *you're* doing here, and it had better be good."

Beth excused herself as soon as she had finished cleaning up the kitchen after dinner. Although Jana's parents were nice, being with them was like being questioned by the gestapo. Since she was the only kid in the family, they were both continually asking her how her day was, how she was doing in this class or that class, what were she and her friends doing . . . all kinds of things.

The attention was starting to drive Beth buggy. *She* wasn't used to it. She swore she would never, ever again complain about her family's ignoring her at home. She hadn't realized how nice it was to have four other kids to share the limelight with until now. She switched on the light over Jana's desk and flipped open Jana's social studies book.

Beth read a page and then paused. Everyone in school thought that Jana and Randy were the world's most perfect couple, and it made Beth feel terrible to know that she had messed things up so badly between them. What could she do to straighten things out? Maybe she should call and see if Randy would come over and give her a chance to explain.

Beth popped out of her chair and ran to the closet. That *wasn't* a bad idea, but if Randy said he'd come right over, she'd better be ready. It would only take him five minutes to ride over on his bike.

She searched through Jana's clothes for something nice. Not the denim outfit; she'd worn that on Saturday. There was a pretty red sweater, and the black pants would go great with it. All she needed was something to add a little flash to the outfit. Where did Jana keep her scarves and stuff like that?

Spotting a boot box on the shelf of the closet,

Beth pulled it down. It was full, so she took it to the desk to look through it. When she opened it, she was disappointed. It was filled with odds and ends and looked more like Jana's keepsake box. She was about to put the lid back on when she noticed an envelope lying on top. For some reason she picked it up and opened it. It was an unfinished letter that read:

> *Dear Father:*
> *I am writing this letter to tell you about Mom and Pink's wedding. I am sure you will be just as happy about it as I am. Pink is a very nice man. It will be nice to have a man around the house to help Mom with things. They are getting married one week from Saturday.*

Jana had never finished it. Beth folded the letter and put it back into its envelope.

Next she picked up a letter that was addressed to Jana and postmarked from Poughkeepsie, New York. It had to be from her father, and Beth couldn't resist reading it.

It was dated during summer vacation before The Fabulous Five had gone into the sixth grade at Mark Twain Elementary. In it Jana's father told Jana he would be coming to pick her up and take her on a super trip out west. Beth remembered how excited Jana had been when she had gotten the letter. She also remembered that Jana's father had never come to get her.

Beth slowly put the letters back in the boot box. Before this evening she hadn't really understood what it was like to be in Jana's situation and why Jana was so confused about what to buy Pink and her father for Father's Day. Pink actually treated Jana nicer than her father did, but she still loved her father.

Beth felt like kicking herself. Not only had she messed up Jana's love life, but she hadn't been understanding like a *real* friend should have been. Well, she told herself firmly, I'm going to make it up to Jana. She put the boot box back on the shelf and started getting dressed.

"Melanie's home!" yelled Jeffy as Katie walked into the Edwardses' house. He ran at her and wrapped his arms around her waist, nearly knocking her over.

"Okay, okay, you little ape," Katie said, laughing. "You don't have to destroy me."

"Play with me, Melanie."

"Hey, I just got home. Give me a chance to get settled."

"Aww," said Jeffy, sticking out his lower lip in a pout.

Katie thought she ought to stop in the kitchen and see Mrs. Edwards before she went to Melanie's room. Besides, she was getting used to being able to grab one of those superfantastic brownies that were always on the counter. She knew Melanie's mother didn't *really* care because the plate never got any emptier.

"Hi, sweetheart," said Mrs. Edwards.

"Hi, Mom." Katie startled herself. She had called Melanie's mother Mom. Being in the Edwardses' house was starting to seem strangely natural.

Before she could think any more about it, Melanie's mother said, "Would you take care of Rainbow? She hasn't been fed and she needs to go outside. I can't take the time right now."

Katie was happy to take care of Rainbow. The calico-colored dog was in the basement and came wiggling and wagging to Katie when she opened the door. Her heart's really in her tail, thought Katie as she hugged the animal.

After she had fed Rainbow and let her out into the backyard, Katie went back to the kitchen to get the brownie she had missed. She was munching away quietly, and watching Mrs. Edwards's dinner preparations, when a loud crash came from the living room.

"*Yoww!*" Jeffy's cry echoed through the house.

Melanie's mother dropped her ladle and ran to see what had happened. Katie was right on her heels.

When they got to the living room, they found Jeffy sitting on the floor and leaning against the television. He was holding both hands to his head.

"What happened?" Mrs. Edwards said as she bent over and picked him up.

"I fell," he whimpered, reaching out for Katie with both arms.

"Fell?" asked his mother as she handed him to Katie.

"Off the TV," Jeffy said as he wrapped his arms around Katie's neck so tightly she thought she was going to choke. "I was playing climb the mountain and I slipped."

Katie pulled his hand away from his head. A bump was starting to rise above the left eye and was almost the size of an egg.

"Oh, dear," said Mrs. Edwards. "That looks terrible. We'd better call the doctor."

Katie held Jeffy and rocked him while his mother made the call. He pressed his head against her shoulder, and now and then a convulsive sob racked his little body.

"The doctor says it's possible that he might have a concussion and that we should watch him closely. Would you put his pajamas on him and get him ready for bed, Melanie? We'll feed him his supper in there, but the *one thing* we mustn't do is let him go to sleep. Someone will have to stay with him."

"I will," said Katie, putting her hand behind his head and pressing him closer to her. He gave another little whimper that nearly broke Katie's heart.

Katie spent the whole evening in Jeffy's room. He wanted to lie back and not eat, but she kept him awake by building a fort out of his mashed potatoes with a gravy moat around it. The peas were the bad soldiers, and Jeffy was the good dragon who ate them all up. Soon she had him giggling. Next she taught him simple card games.

When Mr. and Mrs. Edwards came to check on them, he was wide-awake and having a good time. "I think he can go to sleep now, if he wants to," said Mrs. Edwards.

As they walked down the hall, Mr. Edwards put his arm around Katie and squeezed her shoulder. "You're so good with him, Melanie. No wonder he loves you so much."

Mrs. Edwards smiled at her. "We always know we can count on you when we need help."

Later, as Katie sat in Melanie's room, she thought back over the last few days. It seemed as if everyone came to Melanie for help. Mona did, Dekeisha did, and even Jeffy did when he was hurt. Come to think of it, if Katie had a problem, Melanie would be just about the first person she would think of to ask for help, too.

Katie drew little circles over and over again on the pad in front of her. Even though they were friends, maybe she really hadn't totally understood what kind of person Melanie was. All the people who asked Melanie for help were proof of the kind of heart Melanie had. It was Melanie's heart that had caused her to give Mona the answers to the history questions. Katie knew now that she really hadn't been fair to her.

*   *   *

Melanie scuffed forlornly up the stairs to Christie's room. No one else was home yet, and the Winchells' house was terribly quiet. If only Rainbow were here, she thought. I could hug her and pet her and tell her about all the trouble I've accidentally gotten Christie into. Rainbow would understand, and she would look up at me with those soft, brown eyes of hers and probably wag her tail to try to make me feel better.

She sat down on the edge of Christie's bed, pulling off first her left shoe and then the sock and rubbing the sore place where the hard piece of gravel had been for the entire day. There's actually a bruise on that spot—for all the good that stupid rock did, she thought, peering at a bluish circle on the skin. And Jon's even angrier than he was before.

But Jon was only part of the problem. She had walked around in a daze ever since the honors history test this afternoon and the disastrous way she had let Christie down.

"I never realized before how tough it is to be Christie," she whispered as tears misted her eyes. Then she flopped on her back and stared at the ceiling, still talking to herself. "I guess I never knew how hard she works for her grades or how important they are to her. It's no wonder that she doesn't feel she has time for boys."

Melanie popped up like a jack-in-the-box, sitting poker-straight in the middle of the bed and opening her eyes wide. "Did I say *that*?" she shrieked. "I must be going bananas!"

Slowly Melanie's eyes drifted to the stack of books she had dropped onto Christie's desk. The big gray history book sat on top, looking dull and as heavy as a slab of concrete.

What good would it do to know all that stuff anyway? she wondered. Only a history teacher had to know it. Or someone who lived back then. She giggled, trying to imagine herself in England in the days of King Henry VIII. I certainly wouldn't want *him* for a boyfriend, she thought.

Just then the telephone on her desk rang, piercing the silence and making her jump half a foot off the bed. She scrambled for it and lifted the receiver just as it started to ring a second time. "Hello?"

"Christie, honey. Are you okay?" It was Mrs. Winchell, and she sounded worried.

"Sure, I'm fine," Melanie assured her. "Why?"

The worry was still in Christie's mother's voice. "I just had a call from Miss Jamal, and she said that you were acting strange this afternoon in class and that you . . . that you *failed* your test. She was worried about you, and so am I. Christie, please tell me the truth. Is something wrong?"

"Um . . . well . . ." Melanie began, trying to stall for time while she tried to think of some way to answer.

"Sweetheart, you know you can talk to me about whatever's bothering you. Are you sick? Or did something awful happen at school? You aren't fighting with your friends again, are you?"

"No. Nothing like that," Melanie interjected. "I mean, I'm not fighting with The Fabulous Five. In fact, everything's . . ." She couldn't finish the sentence because tears had filled her throat. How could she possibly tell Mrs. Winchell the truth? She hadn't *just* flunked the test, she wasn't even Christie! She was an imposter. Trapped inside Christie's body so that everybody thought she was Christie. But she wasn't. She was Melanie Edwards, and she couldn't pass an honors history test if her life depended on it.

"Christie! What is it?" Mrs. Winchell's voice had raised a couple of levels from mere worry to near panic. "On second thought, don't say any more. I'll be right home."

A queasy feeling filled the pit of Melanie's stomach as she hung up the phone. Mrs. Winchell would come bursting into the room in a little while wanting to know what was wrong. But Melanie knew she wouldn't be able to tell her the truth. No matter how hard she tried. The words simply wouldn't come. She knew, because she had tried it before.

But if I can't tell her or anyone else and I have to go on being Christie, then I'm going to go on disappointing everybody because I'll flunk my tests and not do *anything* the way Christie would do it. I mean, I'm Melanie Edwards. What else can I do?

Melanie's hand came to rest on the awful history book. There is one thing, she conceded. I mean, I could try. Maybe I could hold things together for Christie until both of us get back to normal—if we ever do.

Opening the book, she turned to the first of the chapters covered on the test today. "I'm going to study these harder than I've ever studied anything in my life. And then I'll explain to Mrs. Win . . . *Mom* . . . that I wasn't feeling well at school today. And maybe, just maybe, she'll help me convince Miss Jamal to let Chris . . . *me* . . . take the test again.

Christie glanced around the Barry dinner table in astonishment, thinking that the scene before her gave new meaning to "feeding time at the zoo." Brian had heaped his plate with three pieces of fried chicken, a mountain of mashed potatoes and gravy, four hot rolls, and three of the smallest green beans he could pick out of the dish. He would never have gotten away with that at my house! Christie thought with an air of superiority.

Brittany, on the other hand, had come to the table announcing that she was on a new diet and that all she could have for dinner on day one was a small raw potato, peeled, and half a cup of plain, low-fat yogurt. *Yuk!* thought Christie as Brittany sliced the potato, which was already turning brown from exposure to the air, and spooned the yogurt over it. It looked disgusting.

She wasn't sure what Todd had on his plate. He

had tossed it all into one pile, stirred everything together, and was shoveling it into his mouth at an
incredible rate of speed. "Gotta hurry," he said between bites. "Guys are waiting."

Alicia had whined and whined that all she wanted
was mashed potatoes and gravy until Mrs. Barry
gave in, making her promise she would eat a big
breakfast the next morning in exchange. Now Alicia
played in the mess with her fork and occasionally
dipped a finger into the gravy when neither of her
parents was looking and held it under her chair for
Agatha to lick.

Christie was aware that no one seemed to notice
that she had not touched a single bite of the food on
her plate. Of course, everyone was too busy. Mr.
Barry's nose was buried in the evening newspaper,
and Mrs. Barry jumped up at least a dozen times
during the meal to put laundry from the washer into
the dryer, to check the frozen cherry pie that was
bubbling in the oven, or to take care of a bunch of
other chores.

"Everything breaks loose at dinnertime," she
complained good-naturedly.

Brittany crunched a bite of raw potato and glared
at Christie. "The telephone's *mine* after dinner, little
sister, so don't think you can get away with tying it
up."

"Hey, it's not *yours*," said Brian, flicking a green
bean at Brittany.

"Children," growled Mr. Barry from behind his newspaper.

"Well, it isn't hers," Brian protested. "It belongs to the family. Besides, there's this new chick in my geometry class, and I told her to call me if she got stuck on any of the problems in tonight's homework. How can she get through if *The Mouth* is babbling into it all night."

"Tough," said Brittany. She stood up and was about to make a mad dash to the wall phone in the kitchen when Christie decided she couldn't stand it any longer.

"Listen, everybody. This is ridiculous. If this whole family would just get organized we could save a lot of trouble."

"Hey, Todd. Pitch me another roll," said Brian. Noticing his mother glaring at him, he added in an exaggerated voice, *"Ple-e-e-ze!"*

Todd slid the roll basket across the table to Brian, completely ignoring Christie. Brittany had stopped momentarily, and Christie thought for an instant that she had gotten Beth's older sister's attention, but she was wrong. Instead, Brittany grabbed the green bean stuck to her sweatshirt and dropped it into Brian's hair and then proceeded to the phone and began dialing.

"Hey, everybody," Christie called in exasperation. "If we just got organized . . . We could assign each person a certain time to use the phone. Then we could all tell our friends that was when they could call. It would work. I know it would."

"See you guys later," Todd called as he wiped the milk mustache off his mouth and bounded for the door.

Brian disappeared an instant later, and then Mr. Barry headed down to the basement, saying he had to look at the furnace. Christie felt totally deflated. Horribly ignored. Nobody listened. It's just the way Beth said it was. Nobody heard a single word I said, she thought. It's as if I'm not even here. Nothing like this ever happened to me before. At my house, everybody listens.

Turning to Mrs. Barry, Christie started to speak again. It was her last chance, and she wanted to make it good.

"Beth, dear," Mrs. Barry said before Christie could utter a sound. "Would you clean up the kitchen? I have to get Alicia into the tub." Then without waiting for an answer, she took Alicia by the hand and left the room, leaving Christie staring openmouthed after her.

CHAPTER

11

Jana glared at both Shawnie and Tony. She had caught them in the act of two-timing Katie, and she wasn't going to let them off the hook. "I think it's despicable that you two are sneaking behind Katie's . . . er, my back," she said.

"Sneaking behind your back? What are you talking about, Katie Shannon?" Shawnie squealed in disbelief.

"This is the third time that I've been by your house and Tony's bike has been out front. If that's not sneaking around, I don't know what is."

Tony looked at her coldly. "You've been by here three times? Were you spying on us?"

134

"Don't change the subject," said Jana, getting angrier.

"I can't believe this," said Shawnie, shaking her head. Then looking at Tony, she said, "I'm going to tell her."

"Don't do it," said Tony.

"She's acting ridiculous, and I'm going to do it."

"I don't want you to," he said.

Jana's head moved back and forth between Shawnie and Tony as they argued. It was like watching a Ping-Pong match, and they were getting her off track. She didn't like it. "There's *nothing* that you can tell me that will make any difference."

Shawnie looked at Jana with a smirk. "Not even if I told you Tony has been doing yard work for my parents, Miss Know-it-all?"

"Yard work?" Jana said, her mouth falling open.

Shawnie crossed her arms and looked down at her from the porch. "Yes, and do you know what, Katie Shannon?"

The question made Jana feel very uneasy. She was afraid of what was coming next.

Shawnie leaned forward to make her point. "He's been working to save money so he could buy *you* a big corsage and take *you* out to eat after the dance."

A blush crawled up Jana's neck, and her face felt suddenly very stiff. She felt as if she were going to melt and dribble right down into her shoes. She dared to take a peek at Tony, who stood looking at her. His face was expressionless.

"Well, I . . ." Jana started, but didn't know what to say.

"So you were spying on Tony?" Shawnie asked, a superior look on her face. "I guess you don't really trust him, do you?"

"I-I, uh . . ." stuttered Jana. To her dismay, Tony got on his bike and rode away.

Christie sat alone in the Barry kitchen surrounded by piles of dirty dishes. Poor Beth! she thought. It's as if she is invisible in her own family. Now I understand why she acts so theatrical all the time. It's the only way she can think of to get attention.

Slowly Christie scraped the dishes and loaded them into the dishwasher. But Beth doesn't have to try to get attention in The Fabulous Five, Christie reasoned. We're all best friends.

She cringed, remembering the trouble they had been having lately. We *used to be* best friends. But for the past few days everyone has been picking on each other and griping about each other. In fact, she reminded herself with a frown, it feels as if we're going to break up.

The thought startled Christie. Last week, before the slumber party at Katie's house, the idea of breaking up hadn't seemed so terrible. Nobody had understood her. They were always criticizing her for studying so much and being so organized.

"And I was just as bad as they were," she whispered to herself. "I criticized all of them, *especially* Beth."

Christie thought about that for a moment. She had been so sure that she could get Beth's life organized. She had absolutely known that if Beth would apply Christie's own logical methods of handling things, Beth's troubles would be over. Or at least most of them, anyway. But it hadn't worked. Brian hadn't listened to her idea about assigning telephone time, or Todd or Alicia. And *forget* Brittany! she thought with disgust.

That only left one alternative. She would have to try to solve one problem the way Beth would do it. Only then would she know if Beth was right, or if she deserved all the criticism she had been getting.

Christie finished cleaning up the kitchen, trying to decide how to put her plan into action. She remembered the story Beth had told them about how, a few months ago, she had finally managed to get her parents' attention by putting on bandages and makeup so that she looked as if she'd been in an accident. When she came stumbling down the stairs in that condition, her mother had almost fainted, but Beth had certainly gotten her attention.

Christie couldn't help chuckling at the thought, but she could never do a thing like that, she reasoned. Still, what could she do?

She washed off the table and the countertops and looked around to be sure she hadn't forgotten anything when she heard a commotion in the upstairs hall.

"Brian, I told you that I get the phone tonight," Brittany was shrieking. "Now hang up and let me have it!"

"Get out of here," Brian yelled. "I can use it if I want to."

By the time Christie had rushed up the stairs, Alicia and Agatha had joined the confusion.

Agatha was running in circles, barking, and Alicia jumped up and down, shouting, "Mommy! Daddy! They're fighting!"

Christie put her hands on her hips and watched Brittany try to grab the receiver out of Brian's hand while he swiped at her, trying to fend her off.

"Come on, guys," Christie called. "Knock it off. All you have to do is take turns."

Nobody paid the slightest attention to her as the fight continued.

"Did you hear me?" she shouted. "I said *take turns*."

"Give me that phone, you little creep!" Brittany yelled. "I have to make a very important call."

Christie's blood was starting to boil. Why wouldn't anybody listen to her?

Because you're Beth, said a little voice inside her brain. Now go ahead and do what Beth would do.

Christie smiled to herself. Then she raised her head high and shouted as loud as she could, *"Fire!"*

Everyone froze in midair, staring at her in disbelief. Even Agatha gave her a puzzled look.

"Fire?" Brian shouted with panic in his voice. "Oh, my gosh! Where?"

Christie stood there looking at the three of them. "I can't believe this," she said. "I've finally gotten your attention."

"The fire!" screamed Brittany.

Christie reached out and took the phone out of Brian's trembling hand. "Oh, there's no fire," she confessed sweetly. "I just needed to use the phone."

Melanie studied late into the night for Christie's honors history test. She had been able to convince Mrs. Winchell that a rotten headache and an upset stomach had caused her to blank out everything she knew during the exam.

"I think it was something I ate because I feel fine now," she had said, knowing she was not exactly telling the truth but believing firmly that it was for a good cause. Besides, I couldn't have told her the truth even if I'd wanted to, she reminded herself. The words wouldn't have come out right.

Mrs. Winchell telephoned Miss Jamal, and the history teacher agreed that, since Christie had been sick, she could take a makeup test the following morning an hour before regular classes began.

Melanie had never felt more relieved in her life.

But she was also nervous. She had to do well on the test for Christie's sake.

She flipped open the book and turned to the first chapter covered on the test. She sighed. She had already read it twice. That was the way she usually prepared for her own tests. But of course her grades weren't nearly as good as Christie's.

"I wonder how Christie would study?" she whispered.

Almost like magic, she remembered a bright yellow highlighter pen she had seen in Christie's desk drawer. Getting it, she began reading the chapter again, highlighting the most important points. There, she thought when she finished the chapter. It will be easy to review for the test. Next she recopied the notes Christie had made in her notebook, remembering that she had heard somewhere that writing things down helped fix them in a person's mind.

She went through each of the three chapters with the highlighter pen and the notebook until she was sure there was nothing about England in the 1500s that she didn't know, and she fell into bed and dropped off to sleep mumbling to herself. "Mary, Queen of Scots, was executed for treason in 1587. The six wives of Henry VIII were Catherine Parr, Ann Boleyn, Catherine . . ."

Miss Jamal was in her classroom when Melanie got there the next morning. It felt strange to walk through the halls an hour before classes and hear her footsteps echo in the stillness. But it felt even

stranger to enter the honors history room and pre-
pare to take a test.

"Good morning, Christie," Miss Jamal said pleasantly. She handed Melanie the test paper and added,
"I'm glad you're feeling better today."

Melanie murmured thanks and got out her pencil.
Then she squared her shoulders and looked cautiously at the test. Had she really studied enough?
Had she missed something important that Christie
would have done?

She couldn't believe her eyes. She knew the answers to the first and the second questions. Her
pulse quickened as she read on down the page. The
questions were different from the test the day before, but it didn't matter. *She knew the answers*. This
was going to be a snap, she thought deliriously, just
as Curtis had said yesterday!

Twenty minutes later she handed in the test. Miss
Jamal looked up from her paperwork and smiled at
Melanie as she took the test from her. "Now that was
more like it," she said, glancing down the page. "I
knew something had to be wrong yesterday when
you did so poorly. I'll have this graded by class time
this afternoon, but it looks as if you may have scored
one hundred."

Melanie was walking on air when she left the
classroom. *One hundred on an honors history test!* It was
more than she could believe. How could I be so
lucky? she asked herself. Then she frowned. I wasn't

lucky. I worked hard for that grade. I studied and I knew the material. And not only that, I feel terrific!

She walked toward her locker, thinking about what a high it was to be making fabulous grades. Me, she wanted to shout, Melanie Edwards—*brain*. But no one would ever know. The new thought depressed her as much as the old one had made her happy. Everyone will think Christie Winchell made one hundred on that test. It isn't fair!

"Melanie Edwards! I hope you think you're funny!" Dekeisha Adams had been waiting for Katie at the school gate, and now she stood in front of her with her hands on her hips and a very angry look on her face.

"What? . . . What's the matter?" asked Katie.

"What's the matter? It's the flirting tips you gave me. They're not worth a darn."

"Why?" asked Katie.

"You told me to be straightforward and tell Don Petry exactly what I think and to let him know I expect to be treated as an equal, and he'd like me. I did that. He asked me to go to Taco Plenty after school yesterday, and when he dribbled taco sauce on his chin, I told him he was uncouth. And *then* I told him about how I thought males and females were equal in every way, and he let me pay for the food and drinks."

"So?" said Katie. "That's not so bad."

"Maybe not, but right after that Marlo Andrews came by, and he left with her. All *she* did was blink her eyes at him. How come you didn't tell me to blink my eyes at him? So much for your flirting tips, Melanie Edwards," she said, tossing a crumpled piece of paper at Katie's feet. "Don will never ask me to the school dance now. See if I ever speak to *you* again." Dekeisha spun on her heel and stormed off.

Katie picked up the paper and unfolded it. It was the tips she had given Dekeisha.

Later, Katie sat in homeroom trying to figure out what had gone wrong. The tips she had given Dekeisha had certainly worked for her with Tony. Why hadn't they worked for Dekeisha? She couldn't figure it out. One thing was for sure, though. Dekeisha was *very* mad at Melanie and Katie was the cause of it.

That meant Katie owed Melanie one more time. First, she hadn't understood how much people asked Melanie for help, and how, out of the goodness of her heart, Melanie never turned them down. She had been all over Melanie for being gullible, but the truth was Melanie just cared a lot about other people. Now, Katie had ruined the friendship between Melanie and Dekeisha. She was going to have to find a way to get Don Petry to ask Dekeisha to the dance. The bell ending the homeroom period startled Katie out of her thoughts.

"Melanie," said Miss Dickinson as Katie passed

her desk on the way out of the room. "Here's a note from Mr. Naset for you."

Katie read the note as she hurried down the hall to her next class. It was addressed to both Melanie and Mona.

Melanie Edwards/Mona Vaughn:

I would appreciate it if the two of you would meet me in my office together right after third period today.

Mr. Naset

He had underlined the word together. What could he want to see Mona and her about at the same time? A shiver went through Katie. Something told her it had to do with the history test.

Beth gathered up all her courage and marched up to Randy Kirwan, who was putting his gym clothes back in his locker. "Hi," she said, flashing him her biggest and brightest smile. First Randy looked happy to see her, then he looked confused, and then his face went blank. "Hi, Jana," he answered.

"I was wondering . . ." Beth said, trying to look as sincere as possible. Jana always said Randy was the kindest and most sincere person in the world, and Beth had to let him see how sincere she was.

"Would you like to . . . *could you* come over tonight for a little while?"

"Are you sure you want me to?" he asked.

"Of course I do," she said.

"What about Keith? It looks as if you're starting to like him now."

"That's part of the reason why I want you to come over," she said softly. "I want to explain about Keith. Things aren't the way you think. In fact, as far as I'm concerned, nothing has changed between you and me."

A smile shone in Randy's eyes and then spread to his lips. "Seven o'clock okay?"

She squeezed his hand and nodded.

CHAPTER

12

*J*ana was so embarrassed and worried about making things worse for Katie that she didn't know what to do. She had immediately apologized to Shawnie for thinking that she and Tony were sneaking around behind Katie's back. Jana had also called Tony as soon as she reached Katie's house, but his mother said he wouldn't come to the phone. Later, she paced back and forth in Katie's room, hoping that Tony would change his mind and call. But he hadn't. Now Jana was sitting in class waiting for the bell to ring so she could dash out into the hall to find Tony and apologize.

Boy, had she messed things up between Katie and

Tony. All the time she had thought that Katie's stubbornness was keeping Katie from seeing that Tony was cheating on her. Well, for once Katie had been right to be stubborn, and Jana was miserable for having meddled in Katie's life. Jana wished with all her heart that she could get back into her own body and Katie into hers so Jana could apologize. She gave a big sigh. She had thought she was being loyal to her friend, but it turned out she was just being dumb.

Jana fingered the paper bag containing the gift-wrapped box and waited for the bell. She crossed her fingers that it would do the trick.

Finally, the bell rang and Jana scurried out of the classroom. Moving quickly, she dodged through the kids and stood on her tiptoes to try to catch sight of Tony. He wasn't at the place where they normally met, so she hurried on. She found him beside the drinking fountain, talking to Bill Soliday and Shane Arrington.

Jana stood where he couldn't help but see her and waited patiently. When he did notice her, she thought . . . hoped was more like it . . . that his eyes softened. He shifted his feet nervously and glanced at her out of the corner of his eye. Finally, he left the others and came over to her.

"Yo," she said in a small voice.

"Yo, Your Honor," he responded.

Reaching into the bag, she pulled out the gift and without saying a word, handed it to him.

"What's this?" he asked.

"Open it. Please," she added.

Tony pulled the red ribbon off the box and then the paper. Inside was a small hangman's noose made out of pink yarn.

"I've been called the hanging judge a few times, so I thought it would be the appropriate thing for you to hang me with for not trusting you." She gave him a little smile. "Usually, I'm very stubborn about things, you know." She thought she saw the corners of his mouth twitch at her remark. "I couldn't really believe you were cheating on me," she continued, "but I panicked. I should have been stubborn in my faith in you. If you forgive me, I promise never ever to doubt you again."

After her speech, Jana stood with her fingers crossed behind her, waiting for Tony to decide Katie's fate. If he decided not to make up, Jana would be miserable for the rest of her life, knowing that it had been her fault.

"Well, Your Honor," he said. "I guess it's kind of nice to know how much you really like me. One thing though."

"What's that?" asked Jana.

"I don't want you to like me so much you buy me a corsage for the dance. I like being different, but not *that* different."

Jana laughed and put her arm through Tony's, and they walked down the hall together.

* * *

Katie and Mona sat in chairs directly in front of Mr. Naset's desk. The teacher had his head down and was using his index fingers to run down two sets of papers. Trying not to be too obvious, Katie strained to see what they were. They looked like tests, and one of them had Melanie's name on it. A terrible sinking feeling filled Katie's stomach.

This was it. Zero hour. Mr. Naset *knew* that Mona had gotten the answers from Melanie, and he was going to accuse them of it. The bad thing was, Katie didn't know what she could do to get Melanie out of this mess. Katie had thought and thought, but she hadn't been able to come up with any kind of plan.

Katie wanted to tell Mr. Naset what it was like to be Melanie and have people asking you for help all the time. She thought she understood Melanie now that she'd been in Melanie's body for four days. Melanie wasn't a cheat. It was her good heart that got her in trouble. But Katie knew she wouldn't be able to say the words. She clenched her fists in frustration at not being able to help her friend.

"Humph." Mr. Naset looked up from his desk and cleared his throat. "I guess you probably know why I called you two in."

Katie nodded and glanced at Mona. Mona looked miserable. Her hands were knotted together in her lap, and she looked as if she were about to cry. Katie wanted to hate Mona for getting Melanie in trouble, but she couldn't. Instead she gritted her teeth and waited for the verdict. Mr. Naset would have to give them both F's on the tests. Would he also fail them for the course?

"These two tests . . ." he began.

"Sir," said Mona in a weak little voice.

He frowned at the interruption. "Yes?"

Mona took a deep breath and tears filled her eyes. "I cheated," she said.

"That's obvious to me," the teacher responded.

"No. What I mean is *I* cheated," she said, her voice sounding braver. "Melanie didn't. I saw Melanie's test lying on the table in study hall, and I looked at it. She didn't know anything about it."

Katie's mouth dropped open. She shut it just in time to keep Mr. Naset from seeing her surprise.

"Ummm." Mr. Naset arched his eyebrows. "This sheds a different light on things. Er, Melanie, would you step out in the hall for a moment while I talk to Mona?"

Katie could hardly stand the suspense as she stood outside the office. Would Mona stick by her story? Should Katie tell Mr. Naset that Melanie *had* given Mona the answers? No. She wouldn't be able to do that because it had been Mona who had gotten Melanie into this mess in the first place. What she would do was keep close track of her warmhearted friend to keep her from getting in this kind of trouble again.

Shortly, the door opened and a red-eyed Mona came out. She gave Katie a weak smile. "I'm sorry, Melanie. I didn't mean to get you in trouble. It's okay now, though. Mr. Naset isn't going to change your grade."

Katie looked sadly at Mona. "What's going to happen to you?"

"I flunked the test and the course. But I was going to do that, anyway, so I'm right back where I started. The really important thing is for you to understand how sorry I am, Melanie. I will *never ever* do anything like that again," she said, raising her right hand. "Melanie, you're a really super person."

You can say that again, thought Katie.

Melanie continued to glow over her good grade in honors history all day. It amazed her that she could do as well as Christie in a class she wasn't even taking. "Maybe I'm really a genius and just don't know it," she murmured, and giggled to herself as she hurried between her third- and fourth-period classes. "Maybe I should sign up for trigonometry next year, or calculus."

"So now you're talking to yourself." Jon's voice boomed over her left shoulder. "What's going on with you, anyway? What's happened to the old Christie?"

Melanie cringed. Was it possible that he knew the truth? But she didn't know what had happened to the old Christie herself, so that was one discussion she didn't want to get involved in.

"You'll believe I'm the old Christie when you see

the grade I got on my honors history test," she bragged. "Mrs. Jamal says it's probably one hundred."

"Okay. I give in. You're the old Christie. Nobody else could do that," he muttered.

Melanie eyed him angrily. She wanted to shout that Melanie Edwards could, but she didn't. She would have to prove to him—and to everybody— just how smart she was later. For now, she had something else to do. She had to put his and Christie's friendship back on track.

She had thought about it a lot since yesterday when he'd caught her limping on the wrong foot. At first she had thought she should use some of the seven tips for flirting. They had always worked for her when she was Melanie. But somehow she couldn't imagine Christie batting her eyes at Jon and telling him that the shirt he was wearing was gorgeous. And she definitely couldn't imagine Jon falling for it.

Actually, Melanie knew there was only one way that Christie would make up with Jon. She would take the logical approach and look him straight in the eye and apologize.

Crossing and uncrossing her fingers three times for luck, she began, "Jon, I'm really sorry that I told you I twisted my ankle when I didn't. The truth is, Mom caught me leaving the house to play tennis and made me go back to my room to study. I tried to call you to tell you that I couldn't meet you, but you had already left for the courts."

Jon looked at her with astonishment. "Why didn't you just say so instead of making up some big story about getting hurt?"

"I thought you might not believe me or that you might get mad," she answered honestly.

"But Christie, that's not like you—"

"I know!" she interrupted. "I'm not sure myself what's been wrong with me lately. It's almost as if someone else has taken over my body." She laughed slyly and then went on, "But I'll tell you one thing, I promise you that I'll be my old self from now on."

"Great," said Jon, giving her a thumbs-up victory sign.

After they went their separate ways to class, Melanie reflected on what she had said to Jon. She really would let Christie be her old self again, at least as long as she was in Christie's skin. Not only that, she had a new respect for Christie as a person. Never again would she criticize her for studying too much or being too serious. It was the perfect way for Christie to be. In fact, Melanie decided, she planned to try a little of the "Christie Winchell Surefire Study Technique" in her own life, if she ever got back to being Melanie Edwards again.

* * *

Beth moved to the couch and sat down beside Randy. Jana's mother and Pink were in the kitchen playing Scrabble, and Beth and Randy had the living room all to themselves.

"Want to watch TV?" asked Randy. "There's a Pee-wee Herman movie on."

Beth shook her head. "No. I'd rather talk." She snuggled up next to him, and he put his arm around her. It still felt strange, but she was doing it for Jana's sake.

"I don't suppose you want to make popcorn," he said.

She looked at him. There was a mischievous gleam in his eye. "Actually, I was *really* thinking about making us a pot-roast dinner instead," she said, giggling. "You know, with potatoes and carrots and all that stuff. It shouldn't take more than a few hours."

"I could make some homemade ice cream while you're doing that," he said, laughing. "Especially since we don't have anything *else* we'd rather be doing."

"Well . . . there is something else I'd rather do than cook," she said.

"Oh? What's that?" Randy asked.

"Just this." She reached up and pulled his head down to her. As she kissed him, she thought, this one's for you, Jana, wherever you are.

* * *

Christie was too antsy to pay attention in any of Beth's classes. A crazy idea was beginning to take over her brain.

It had all started the night before when she understood for the first time why Beth behaved the way she did, always showing off and being theatrical. Beth really did need more attention than she got in that loony-tunes family of hers. It was no wonder she wore wild and crazy clothes and wanted to be an actress where she could stand in the center of the stage and receive the applause of the audience. It made her feel noticed and appreciated.

Christie winced at the painful memory of how she had criticized Beth and told her that she should be a little quieter and less dramatic some of the time. In fact, she had said those very words to Beth at the slumber party on Friday night. She hadn't thought too much about it before because they had all been criticizing each other. But now that she understood Beth, she desperately wished that she could stop being Beth and and get back to being her old self so that she could make up with Beth and tell her that she had been wrong.

"Hey, Beth. Are you going to sit in here all day?"

Startled, Christie looked up to see Alexis Duvall standing in the doorway of the Family Living classroom where all the other seats were empty.

"The bell rang, dummy," Alexis teased.

"Wow. Thanks," said Christie, scrambling to her feet. "I must have been daydreaming."

She daydreamed in her next class, too, remembering how The Fabulous Five had quarreled all through Katie's slumber party, picking on each other's faults.

"I was definitely the one who griped about Beth," she murmured as she watched Miss Dickinson write the English assignment on the board. "I really climbed all over her, and now I'm in her body."

Absently Christie doodled on her notebook paper, drawing neat little boxes and triangles, which she had read somewhere was the product of a logical mind. But being in Beth's skin is anything but logical! she thought. Still, the more she thought about it, the more she was convinced that there might be a sort of logical explanation to how it came about.

"It was the slumber party! That was when everything changed!" She whispered the words so loudly that Joel Murphy, who sat directly in front of her, turned around and raised an eyebrow.

Ignoring him, she thought about the slumber party. She had gone to sleep as herself, but she had awakened the next morning as Beth. *Had the same thing happened to the others?* The idea made her shoot to attention as if someone had poked her in the ribs. They had all been criticizing each other. So maybe—just maybe—they had all been switched around just as she and Beth had.

But who is in my body? she wanted to shout. Beth? she wondered. Had they simply traded? No, she thought a moment later. Beth wasn't griping at me that night. She was letting Jana have it.

Melanie! Oh, no! thought Christie. It was Melanie who was telling me that I'm too uptight all the time. Good grief. If she's in my skin, what has she done to my life? She's probably flunked my honors history test!

As the day wore on and Christie thought about the slumber party, she was more convinced that that that was where things had changed, and that each of The Fabulous Five had awakened in someone else's skin.

If that's really what happened, she decided, there just might be a logical way to change things back. What if we had another slumber party at Katie's house? But would it work? Could it possibly let her be Christie Winchell again?

She was still asking herself the same questions when she stood at her locker after school. What other choice was there? It *would* work. It absolutely had to. And the sooner, the better.

"I'll talk to Katie and convince her that she *has* to have another slumber party," Christie said resolutely as she banged the locker door shut. "And I'll tell her that it *has* to be on Friday night, and *only* The Fabulous Five can come."

Laughing out loud, she ran to find her friend.

CHAPTER

13

"I'll get it!" called Jana as she ran to the door.

"Katie, slow down," said Willie. "I've never seen you more excited about having your friends over for a slumber party. All I ask is that you remember to go to sleep at a reasonable hour."

"We will, Mom." Jana laughed.

Jana was pleased that Beth had come to her and suggested that The Fabulous Five have another slumber party on Friday. She had also insisted that it be at Katie's house just like the last one. The more Jana thought about the idea, the better she liked it. It was like visiting the scene of the crime, since that was when she had somehow gotten mixed up in

Katie's body. Maybe she could begin to understand what had happened at the last slumber party if they reenacted that night.

"Hi," said Melanie as she pulled her pink and white sleeping bag through the doorway. Melanie looked around the house as if she were seeing it for the first time.

Just then, Willie walked into the room. "Hello, Melanie. How are you?"

Melanie gulped and said, "Hello, Mrs. Shannon," in a low voice.

"Why don't you take your things to my room?" said Jana. "I'll wait here. I hear someone else coming."

Christie and Beth arrived together. It struck Jana as funny that Beth was wearing jeans, a blouse with a tailored collar, and a conservative cardigan sweater. She was even wearing tiny little stud earrings instead of the big flamboyant hoops that she usually wore. On the other hand, Christie had the shoelaces to her sneakers untied, and her hair wasn't brushed as neatly as usual.

When the imposter Jana arrived, the real Jana in Katie's body looked at her closely. Things had been such a mess during the week, with her problems with Tony and all, that she hadn't really had time to observe the fake Jana for more than just a few minutes. She looks exactly like me, thought Jana, and talks like me. A feeling of resentment came over her as she remembered this other girl's going on a date with Randy. What had the two of them been doing all week? she wondered.

"The others are in my room," said Jana in her best Katie Shannon voice. "You go on in while I order a couple of deep-dish, pepperoni, green pepper, and mushroom pizzas to be delivered."

As soon as she had put on her pajamas and settled into Beth's sleeping bag, Christie looked across the room at the girl in her own body, wondering for the hundredth time who it was. Could it possibly be Melanie? She looked closely at the other girl, who was nonchalantly twirling a strand of blond hair around a finger. I'll put her to the test, Christie thought.

"So, how did your honors history test go?" she asked the other Christie.

"Great, Beth. Thanks for asking. I made one hundred."

Christie sank back against her pillow in relief. It couldn't be Melanie. Not if she made one hundred.

"It's been a crazy week," said Katie. "I almost broke up with Tony, but thank goodness, I came to my senses."

"The same thing almost happened to me," said Jana. "Randy was mad at me for a while, but we made up."

"I know you'll never believe this," Melanie said, and giggled, "but for once in my life my problems had nothing to do with boys. I almost got in trouble with Mr. Naset for helping Mona a little more than I should have on a test."

"You cheated?" asked the fake Christie.

"Not exactly," Melanie said, looking down at the floor.

The real Christie pushed an empty pizza box aside and snuggled deeper into Beth's sleeping bag and listened to the others talking. She liked this slumber party better than the one the week before. No one was fighting this time, or picking on anyone else. In fact, every one of The Fabulous Five was quieter than usual.

Were they each thinking the same thing she was? That something had happened at their party a week ago and that the only way to get back to normal was to have another slumber party? It seemed as if they were looking at each other a lot.

"I know it's only ten o'clock, but I'm getting awfully sleepy," said Jana, stretching and yawning.

"Gosh, me, too," said Melanie. "In fact, I can hardly keep my eyes open."

Christie pulled the sleeping bag up under her chin and glanced around at the others. No one was behaving as if it were a normal slumber party. In fact, no one had even suggested that they get a video to watch. And now they were all acting as if they were ready to fall asleep. "Maybe we should turn off the lights and say good-night," she offered.

Christie lay awake for a long time. She wanted to

go to sleep, but she couldn't. What if she woke up the next morning only to find that she was still Beth? What would she do then? She didn't *want* to be Beth anymore. Beth was a different person with her own way of doing things. What she really wanted was to be Christie Winchell, *herself.*

Finally, after tossing and turning for what seemed like hours, she drifted off to sleep.

Melanie awoke the next morning when a slice of sunlight stabbed her in the eye. She raised her arms above her head, stretching as far as she could and trying to wake up her entire body. That's funny, she thought. My legs feel too short. If it hadn't taken too much energy, she would have laughed at the thought. That's silly, she told herself. After all, they're *my* legs.

Instantly her eyes popped wide open, and she sat up with a start. My legs *are* short. It was Christie's legs that were long. Cautiously she took a strand of hair and held it out in front of her face. It was back to being reddish brown instead of blond. Melanie grabbed her pillow in her arms and smothered a giggle. It was too good to be true. No more honors history tests. No more pressure from Christie's parents to make straight A's. No more worries over hurting Jon's feelings. She was home free! Back to being *herself.*

She looked around the floor at the room full of

sleeping girls. Was it possible that they had all been in the wrong bodies the same as she had? Down deep she knew that they had. She had begun to suspect it a couple of days ago. So surely they were back to normal, too.

"Hey, everybody. Wake up!" she shouted. "Look at me. I'm Melanie Edwards again!"

Heads popped up from sleeping bags all around the room. Instantly the room was filled with happy chatter.

"I can't believe it! I'm back in my own body!" shrieked Beth.

"Me, too! Me, too!" called Jana.

By this time, Melanie had one arm in the air and was clutching her sleeping bag with the other as she jumped up and down singing, "I'm Melanie Edwards," over and over again.

Just then Beth began jumping around in her sleeping bag, too, and the two friends bunny-hopped over to each other and began to hug.

"Make room for me!" cried Katie, throwing her arms around Beth and Melanie, and in just about a split second the five were hugging and laughing and jumping up and down.

"You won't believe this," said Melanie when things had quieted down a little bit. "I had the craziest dream. I dreamed that I was you, Christie. I even made one hundred on your honors history test."

Everyone started grinning and patting Melanie on the back.

"Way to go," said Christie.

Melanie got a sheepish look on her face. "I told you I got one hundred on the history test in my dream, Christie. What I didn't tell you was that I flunked it the first time. Your mother and Mrs. Jamal thought I . . . you . . . were sick and let me take it over again. That's when I made one hundred. I couldn't believe it, even though it was a dream. Me, making one hundred on any test. It felt so great that I'm going to do some of the things you do to study from now on."

"I had the same kind of dream," offered Christie, turning to Beth. "I dreamed I woke up at the slumber party in your body and I was you for a whole week. Now I can understand why you need attention. Do you know I dreamed that I had to call a fire drill at your house to get everyone to stop and listen to me?" Everyone laughed.

"And I dreamed I was Jana," confessed Beth, looking at Jana and her face turning sad. "Jana, I want to apologize for telling you that you didn't have any reasons to gripe. I've been letting myself get so busy on the dance committees that I didn't have time to listen to you like I should. I think I understand a little better what it's like to be you, now that I've dreamed I was you. If you'd let me, I'd like to help you pick out Father's Day presents for Pink and your dad." Jana got tears in her eyes and squeezed Beth's hand.

"I dreamed I was Melanie," Katie chimed in.

"*You* were *me!*" shrieked Melanie. "I don't believe it."

"Believe it," Katie said emphatically, rolling her eyes. "Thank goodness it was all a dream. Otherwise you'd have a problem."

"What kind of problem?" asked Melanie.

Katie cringed. "I goofed things up in my dream and Dekeisha was mad at you."

"Mad at me? What for?" demanded Melanie.

"Well . . . she asked me if I could help her get Don Petry to ask her for a date to the dance by giving her some tips on flirting. I found your flirting tips, but I decided not to use them and made up two of my own. Because of my tips, she told Don he was uncouth and she ended up paying for their tacos. Just before I woke up, she decided that she's not speaking to you anymore."

The others broke into laughter and started falling all over each other. Beth, who still had her feet in her sleeping bag, lost her balance and grabbed Christie. They both ended up on the floor.

Katie looked at Melanie very seriously. "One thing that I didn't understand about you before I had this dream, Mel, is how often people come to you for help. Everybody thinks you're the most understanding person in the world."

"Now it's my turn," said Jana. "Katie, I thought that you were just being stubborn when you wouldn't listen to me when I told you I saw Tony's bike at Shawnie's. In my dream, I nearly ruined your romance with Tony when I accused him of cheating on you. I guess sometimes it pays to be stubborn."

Suddenly everyone grew quiet.

"We all had the same dream," Jana said, just above a whisper.

Melanie nodded. "That has to be it," she replied. "There isn't any other explanation."

"This is amazing," said Beth. "We all had the same kind of experiences in each other's body. We tried to solve each other's problems using our own methods and personalities, and it didn't work for any of us. At least it sounds as if we all know a little more about each other than we did before the dream."

"Okay, then," said Katie. "Now that we know that we all had one big dream and we all understand each other better, what do we do about it?"

"Well, I don't have to worry about Dekeisha's being mad at me, for one thing," giggled Melanie.

"Seriously, though, we've always been totally best friends," said Jana. "Maybe we've started taking each other too much for granted lately."

"I think that's it," said Christie. "I've always cared a lot about you, Beth, but I guess I quit listening to you without even meaning to."

"I agree. That's the problem we've all had," said Katie. "We started picking at each other over little, unimportant things, and we forgot why we call ourselves The Fabulous Five. We should have remembered the great things about each other that made us like one another in the first place, and how we've always tried our best to understand each other because we cared, and then we did our best to help."

"Right," said Jana. "That dream was the best thing that ever happened to us. It reminded us of how *fabulous* it is to be The Fabulous Five."

"Hey," cried Beth. "We can even have new T-shirts made that say 'I'm Fabulous' across the front. Then everyone at Wakeman Junior High will know how special our friendship really is."

The five girls raised their hands and slapped them together in a circle. *"The FABULOUS Five forever!"* they all yelled. Then they joined hands and marched downstairs for breakfast.

CHAPTER

14

*P*articles of light from a big glass ball hanging overhead chased each other around the dimly lit Wakeman Junior High gymnasium as couples danced to the music of The Dreadful Alternatives. Jana was wearing a dark-green dress with bows at the shoulders that went perfectly with her brown, shoulder-length hair. Beth's dress was hot pink with matching headband, while Katie was dressed in dark red and had a gorgeous corsage pinned to her dress with streamers that hung below her waist. Melanie's soft-blue dress with a lace collar matched her huge blue eyes, and Christie had on a simple gold outfit. The girls were standing at the edge of the dance floor waiting for Randy, Keith, Tony, Shane, and Jon.

"Gee, I'm glad you came, Christie," said Jana. "The dance wouldn't have been the same without you."

"Me, too," said Christie. "I think it would have been horrible to stay at home while you were all here."

"Hey, there's Dekeisha with Don Petry," Beth said. As the couple danced past them, Dekeisha waved.

"Did you help her get a date with Don, Melanie?" asked Christie.

"Have my flirting tips ever failed?" Melanie asked with a big smile.

"Not for you, anyway," Katie teased.

"That's a beautiful corsage you've got on, Katie," said Jana. "It looks expensive."

Katie beamed at her. "I told Tony that, but he said he'd been saving his money and wanted to buy it for me. He's also taking me to a restaurant after the dance."

"Lucky . . ." said Melanie.

"I know," responded Katie.

"And she's stubborn enough to keep him, no matter what dumb things certain people might say," Jana said, smiling at her friend. Katie smiled back, pleased.

"I think Shane looks really neat in his tuxedo," said Melanie. "And he's a *great* master of ceremonies. I couldn't believe it when he took his iguana, Igor, out of the box and it had on a black bow tie and a little top hat."

"I know," Christie said, laughing. "Everyone went wild."

"Oh, look. Here comes Mona," said Beth.

Mona walked up, leading Matt Zeboski by the hand. "Hi, everybody."

"Gee, you look nice, Mona," said Melanie.

"Thanks," Mona said shyly. "Melanie, I was wanting to talk to you. We've got a history test on Monday, and I was wondering if—"

Katie stepped in quickly. "If someone can help you study for it, Mona? *Both* Melanie and I can help you, can't we, Melanie? Why don't the two of you come over to my house tomorrow afternoon, and we'll study together?"

"Oh. Okay," said Mona. "That's nice of you to offer, Katie."

"No problem," answered Katie. "I'd just like to help."

As Mona towed Matt off to see someone else, Melanie winked at Katie. "You're fabulous."

"I know," Katie said, laughing.

"Oh, look," said Jana. "Here come the boys. Maybe now we can dance."

"What have you girls been doing while we've been gone?" asked Randy.

"Oh . . . just being fabulous," said Jana.

The rest of The Fabulous Five smiled at each other. As The Dreadful Alternatives started a slow dance, they took their dates by the hand and led them out into the shimmering light.

ABOUT THE AUTHOR

Betsy Haynes, the daughter of a former newswoman, began scribbling poetry and short stories as soon as she learned to write. A serious writing career, however, had to wait until after her marriage and the arrival of her two children. But that early practice must have paid off, for within three months Mrs. Haynes had sold her first story. In addition to a number of magazine short stories and the Taffy Sinclair series, Mrs. Haynes is also the author of *The Great Mom Swap* and its sequel, *The Great Boyfriend Trap.* She lives in Colleyville, Texas, with her husband, who is also an author.

Meet Taffy Sinclair!

If you're a fan of The Fabulous Five series, you'll love the Taffy Sinclair books by Betsy Haynes. That's where Jana, Katie, Christie, Melanie, and Beth form The Fabulous Five in order to keep up with the snootiest (and prettiest) girl in their class—Taffy Sinclair. In these funny stories about The Fabulous Five's adventures before they start junior high school, Taffy Sinclair stops at nothing to outdo Jana and the rest of The Fabulous Five. She tries blackmail, starring in a TV soap opera, and even being friendly, but together The Fabulous Five manage to stay one step ahead of their archenemy, the perfectly gorgeous, perfectly awful Taffy Sinclair!

You can follow The Fabulous Five's fifth- and sixth-grade adventures and find out how it all started in these Taffy Sinclair books available from Bantam Skylark Books:

The Against Taffy Sinclair Club
It was bad enough when Taffy Sinclair was just a pretty face. But now that she's developing faster than Jana Morgan and her four best friends, it's all-out war! What Jana and her friends don't know is that even the best-laid plans can backfire suddenly.

Taffy Sinclair Strikes Again
It's time gorgeous Taffy Sinclair had a little competition. That's why Jana Morgan and her friends form The Fabulous Five, a self-improvement club. But when the third club meeting ends in disaster, Jana finds she has four new enemies. And with enemies like these, there's only one friend worth having . . . Taffy Sinclair!

Taffy Sinclair, Queen of the Soaps
Taffy Sinclair has done it again! This time, she's landed a role in a soap opera, playing a beautiful girl on her deathbed. Is there any way at all for The Fabulous Five to fight back against Taffy Sinclair, the TV star?

Taffy Sinclair and the Romance Machine Disaster

Taffy Sinclair is furious when she finds out that Jana Morgan is the first girl at Mark Twain Elementary School to have a date with Randy Kirwan. Taffy gets her revenge when their sixth-grade teacher conducts a computer matchup game and nine other girls beside Jana turn out to be a "perfect match" with Randy!

Blackmailed by Taffy Sinclair

Taffy Sinclair has never been *this* terrible! When Jana finds a wallet that turns out to be stolen property, and Taffy catches her with it, Taffy makes Jana her personal slave. Jana is stuck serving Taffy her lunch, carrying her books, and worst of all, being her friend, until the rest of The Fabulous Five can help her prove her innocence.

Taffy Sinclair, Baby Ashley, and Me

Jana and Taffy are on their way to the principal's office after having an argument in class when they find an abandoned baby on the front steps of the school. The two girls rescue baby Ashley, and become overnight celebrities. But can two archenemies share the limelight?

Taffy Sinclair and the
Secret Admirer Epidemic

Jana Morgan has been receiving love notes from a secret admirer! And when Taffy Sinclair finds out, she's sure to be jealous. The Fabulous Five set out to uncover the identity of Jana's secret admirer . . . and uncover a big surprise instead.

Taffy Sinclair and the Melanie Make-Over

When Taffy Sinclair tells Melanie about a new modeling school, Melanie talks The Fabulous Five into signing up. Soon Melanie is spending lots of time with Taffy Sinclair, who's promised to get Melanie professional modeling jobs. The Fabulous Five know Taffy's up to something. . . . Can they win Melanie back when Taffy's holding out the lure of a glamorous modeling career?

The Truth About Taffy Sinclair

Taffy finally gets her chance to tell the story of the rivalry between her and The Fabulous Five. It's the last week of sixth grade at Mark Twain Elementary School, and all the students are cleaning out their lockers. When some of the boys switch around everyone's belongings, most of the kids think the prank is funny. For Taffy Sinclair, however, it's no laughing matter. Her personal diary is missing, and now the whole school will learn the truth about Taffy Sinclair!

Now Taffy Sinclair is back, in a book all her own titled *Taffy Sinclair Goes to Hollywood*.

Here is a scene that takes place *before* Taffy goes to Hollywood:

By the time Saturday morning arrived, and Taffy and her mother rode the commuter train into New York City, Taffy was so excited that she could scarcely breathe. She had done lots of auditions for television commercials, but this was her first movie audition. Her biggest break.

Channing Crandall *had* liked her improvisation. Maybe she would get the part and go to Hollywood, after all. The thought made her tingle with excitement.

They took a cab to the building on Fifth Avenue where the audition would be held. It was ten minutes to one when they arrived, and Taffy's audition was set for one o'clock.

"Go on, honey. Go on in," her mother urged.

Taffy slowly opened the door to the waiting room and went inside. There were at least a dozen girls already there with their mothers, and more than half of them were standing because there weren't enough chairs. Taffy looked around and started to panic. Almost all of them were brunettes! There was only one other blonde, and she wasn't really a blonde. Her hair was medium brown with streaks of blond. Why am I here? she wanted to cry. There must be a mistake!

Mrs. Sinclair had noticed it, too. She bent close to Taffy's ear and whispered, "Don't worry, sweetheart. We can always dye your hair if you get the part. Remember, Mr. Crandall liked you. Just be yourself and do your best."

Taffy took a deep breath and crossed the room

to the desk, aware that everyone was looking her over, sizing up the competition, and definitely noticing that she had blond hair. She quickly put her name on the union sign-up sheet and handed her résumé to the smiling woman behind the desk.

"Here are your sides, sweetie," said the woman. "You are auditioning for the role of Tiffany Stafford." She handed Taffy a couple of pages from a script that she would be using in the audition and then turned back to her typewriter. She hadn't even seemed to notice that Taffy was a blonde.

"Thanks," murmured Taffy. This was really it. Behind her, she could hear some of the other girls talking together.

"I did *six* auditions this week," a short brunette with huge brown eyes was saying. "My agent says I'll probably get so many offers that the producers will have to bid on me."

"But aren't you putting on a little weight?" asked a slender brown-haired girl standing next to her. "I would think being overweight would limit the number of parts you could play."

Taffy winced at the girls' catty remarks. This was really cutthroat competition—at least in the waiting room. She clutched the sides and looked for a place to stand where she could have some privacy. She had to forget about the other girls and the color of her hair and study the lines she would be reading for Channing Crandall. What if she got them wrong? Or got her tongue twisted? What if he was sorry he had invited her to audition? She remembered what Merry Chase had taught them in acting class: *"Don't memorize the lines because then if you forget them you'll blow the audition. Just get familiar enough with them so that you won't have to keep your eyes glued to the page."*

Taffy picked out the speeches that belonged to Tiffany Stafford and tried to study the lines, but she couldn't concentrate. Her eyes kept darting nervously to the door beside the secretary's desk. It was the door to the audition room, and every so often a brunette would come out, and then the secretary would stand and read off the name of the next girl on the list.

Taffy peered over the top of her sides, watching the faces of the girls coming out for clues to how the auditions were going. Not one of them was smiling.

A chair scraped across the floor. "Taffy Sinclair," called the secretary.

Taffy froze for an instant, but she could feel the eyes of all the other girls on her. All those brunettes who wanted the part as badly as she did. All of them hoping she would panic and run away without even auditioning. Well, she wasn't going to give them that satisfaction. She squared her shoulders and went to the audition-room door. Then she opened it and walked in. She could hear her heart pounding in her ears. Channing Crandall was standing in the center of the dimly lit room talking to the man behind the video camera. In front of the camera was a pool of light, and Taffy knew from experience that was where she would stand.

"Come on in, Taffy," the casting director said cordially, his silver hair catching the light. "It's good to see you again."

Tossing one last frantic look over her shoulder at her mother who had to stay in the waiting room, she closed the door and tried to return Channing Crandall's smile. Her mouth felt starch-stiff. Do I look scared? Will he be able to tell how nervous I am? She moved into the light and faced the camera before she could lose her nerve.

"Before you begin," said the casting director, "let me tell you a little about the story we are filming. *Nobody Likes Tiffany Stafford* is the story of beautiful Tiffany whose life is made miserable by three best friends who despise her. They do everything they can to turn the rest of the school against her."

Taffy tried to keep her mouth from dropping open and from letting the shock she was feeling show on her face. NOBODY LIKES TIFFANY STAFFORD! she wanted to shout. That sounds like my life in Mark Twain Elementary when Jana Morgan and her friends had a club against me called The Against Taffy Sinclair Club!

What happens when Taffy gets the part of Tiffany Stafford and goes to Hollywood?
Find out in *Taffy Sinclair Goes to Hollywood*, coming to your bookstore soon!

ENTER BANTAM BOOKS' BEST FRIENDS 4-EVER SWEEPSTAKES

OFFICIAL RULES:

1. No Purchase is Necessary. Enter by picking up a copy of The Fabulous Five Super #1: THE FABULOUS FIVE IN TROUBLE and TAFFY GOES TO HOLLYWOOD, finding the words "BEST FRIENDS" in the back of the Fabulous Five Super #1: and the words "4-EVER" in the back of TAFFY GOES TO HOLLYWOOD, and mailing the whole message along with the completed Official Entry Form to:

**BEST FRIENDS 4-EVER
SWEEPSTAKES
BANTAM BOOKS,
YR MARKETING
666 FIFTH AVENUE
NEW YORK, NEW YORK 10103**

You may also enter the Sweepstakes by handprinting your name, address, and date of birth on a plain 3" x 5" card along with the message and sending the card to the same address.

1 Grand Prize: The Grand Prize winner will be visited at their school by Betsy Haynes, the author of The Fabulous Five and Taffy Sinclair books.

20 First Prizes: Each First Prize winner will receive five BEST FRIENDS 4-EVER T-shirts (Approximate retail value: $40)

25 Second Prizes: Each second prize winner will receive a boxed set of Taffy Sinclair books (Approximate retail value: $11)

3. All completed entries must be received by Bantam no later than October 1, 1990. Winners will be chosen by Bantam's Young Readers Marketing Department in a random drawing from all entries received on or about November 1, 1990 and will be notified by mail on or about December 1, 1990. Bantam's decision is final and binding. Winners have 30 days from date of notice in which to accept their prize award or an alternate winner will be chosen. A prize won by a minor will be awarded in the name of a parent or legal guardian. Odds of winning depend on the number of completed entries received. All prizes will be awarded. Enter as often as you wish, but each entry must be handwritten and mailed separately. No prize substitution, mechanically reproduced entries, or transfers allowed. Limit one prize per household or address. Bantam is not responsible for incomplete or lost or misdirected entries.

4. Prize winners and their parents or legal guardians may be required to execute an Affidavit of Eligibility and Promotional Release supplied by Bantam. Entering the sweepstakes constitutes permission for use of winner's name, address and likeness for publicity and promotional purposes, with no additional compensation. If permission is necessary in order for Betsy Haynes to visit the Grand Prize winner at their school, the Grand prize winner's parent or legal guardian will be responsible for securing such permission.

5. Employees of Bantam Books, Bantam Doubleday Dell Publishing Group, Inc., their subsidiaries and affiliates, and their immediate family members are not eligible to enter this sweepstakes. This sweepstakes is open to residents of the U.S. and Canada, excluding the Province of Quebec, and is void wherever prohibited or restricted by law. If a Canadian resident, the winner will be required to correctly answer a time-limited arithmetical skill-testing question in order to receive a prize. Taxes, if any, are the winner's sole responsibility.

6. For a list of the winners, send a stamped, self-addressed envelope entirely separate from your entry to BEST FRIENDS 4-EVER SWEEPSTAKES WINNERS LIST, Bantam Books, YR Marketing, 666 Fifth Avenue, 23rd Floor, New York, New York 10103. The winners list will be available after February 1, 1991.

BEST FRIENDS
4-EVER

Friends are special. That's what The
Fabulous Five is all about. Even Taffy Sinclair
understands the importance of friends!

Enter the super fabulous
BEST FRIENDS 4-EVER sweepstakes—
Win a visit by Betsy Haynes to YOUR school!

If you're the Grand Prize winner, you will be visited
at your school by Betsy Haynes, the famous author
of The Fabulous Five and Taffy Sinclair books!
Imagine the excitement in the halls!

Just pick up a copy of TAFFY GOES TO HOLLYWOOD and THE FABU-
LOUS FIVE SUPER #1: THE FABULOUS FIVE IN TROUBLE. In the back of
each book, you will find half of the BEST FRIENDS 4-EVER message. Mail
us the two halves along with the official Entry Form, and we'll enter your
name in the BEST FRIENDS 4-EVER Sweepstakes drawing. See official
rules for alternate means of entry.

MORE GREAT PRIZES!

Twenty First Prize winners will each receive a great
Fab Five T-shirt for them and FOUR of their friends!
Twenty five Second Prize winners will each receive
a boxed set of Taffy Sinclair books. Enter now!

Mail your entries to:
BEST FRIENDS 4-EVER SWEEPSTAKES
BANTAM BOOKS, YR MARKETING
666 Fifth Avenue, New York, NY 10103

BEST FRIENDS 4-EVER OFFICIAL ENTRY FORM

NAME:_____BIRTH DATE:_____
ADDRESS:_____
CITY:_____STATE:_____ZIP:_____

NAME & ADDRESS OF THE STORE WHERE YOU
LEARNED ABOUT SWEEPSTAKES

_____
_____

AN152

From Bantam-Skylark Books
IT'S

From Betsy Haynes, the bestselling author of the Taffy Sinclair books, comes THE FABULOUS FIVE. Follow the adventures of Jana Morgan and the rest of THE FABULOUS FIVE in Wakeman Jr. High.

☐	SEVENTH-GRADE RUMORS (Book #1)	15625-X	$2.75
☐	THE TROUBLE WITH FLIRTING (Book #2)	15633-0	$2.75
☐	THE POPULARITY TRAP (Book #3)	15634-9	$2.75
☐	HER HONOR, KATIE SHANNON (Book #4)	15640-3	$2.75
☐	THE BRAGGING WAR (Book #5)	15651-9	$2.75
☐	THE PARENT GAME (Book #6)	15670-5	$2.75
☐	THE KISSING DISASTER (Book #7)	15710-8	$2.75
☐	THE RUNAWAY CRISIS (Book #8)	15719-1	$2.75
☐	THE BOYFRIEND DILEMMA (Book #9)	15720-5	$2.75
☐	PLAYING THE PART (Book #10)	15745-0	$2.75
☐	HIT AND RUN (Book #11)	15746-9	$2.75
☐	KATIE'S DATING TIPS (Book #12)	15748-5	$2.75
☐	THE CHRISTMAS COUNTDOWN (Book #13)	15756-6	$2.75
☐	SEVENTH-GRADE MENACE (Book #14)	15763-9	$2.75
☐	MELANIE'S IDENTITY CRISIS (Book #15)	15775-2	$2.75
☐	THE HOT-LINE EMERGENCY (Book #16)	15781-7	$2.75
☐	CELEBRITY AUCTION (Book #17)	15784-1	$2.75
☐	TEEN TAXI (Book #18)	15794-9	$2.75
☐	THE BOYS-ONLY CLUB (Book #19)	15809-0	$2.75
☐	SUPER EDITION #1 BREAKING UP	15814-7	$2.95

Buy them at your local bookstore or use this page to order:

Bantam Books, Dept. SK28, 414 East Golf Road, Des Plaines, IL 60016

Please send me the items I have checked above. I am enclosing $_____ (please add $2.00 to cover postage and handling). Send check or money order, no cash or C.O.D.s please.

Mr/Ms _____

Address _____

City/State _____ Zip _____

SK28-8/90

Please allow four to six weeks for delivery
Prices and availability subject to change without notice.

Taffy Sinclair is perfectly gorgeous and totally stuck-up. Ask her rival Jana Morgan or anyone else in the sixth grade of Mark Twain Elementary. Once you meet Taffy, life will **never** be the same.

Don't Miss Any of the Terrific Taffy Sinclair Titles from Betsy Haynes!

- [ ] 15712 **THE AGAINST TAFFY SINCLAIR CLUB** $2.75
- [ ] 15693 **BLACKMAILED BY TAFFY SINCLAIR** $2.75
- [ ] 15604 **TAFFY SINCLAIR AND THE MELANIE MAKEOVER** $2.75
- [ ] 15644 **TAFFY SINCLAIR AND THE ROMANCE MACHINE DISASTER** $2.75
- [ ] 15714 **TAFFY SINCLAIR AND THE SECRET ADMIRER EPIDEMIC** $2.75
- [ ] 15713 **TAFFY SINCLAIR, BABY ASHLEY AND ME** $2.75
- [ ] 15647 **TAFFY SINCLAIR, QUEEN OF THE SOAPS** $2.75
- [ ] 15645 **TAFFY SINCLAIR STRIKES AGAIN** $2.75
- [ ] 15607 **THE TRUTH ABOUT TAFFY SINCLAIR** $2.75

Follow the adventures of Jana and the rest of **THE FABULOUS FIVE** in a new series by Betsy Haynes.

— — — — — — — — — — — — — — — — — —

Bantam Books, Dept. SK26, 414 East Golf Road, Des Plaines, IL 60016

Please send me the items I have checked above. I am enclosing $_____ (please add $2.00 to cover postage and handling). Send check or money order, no cash or C.O.D.s please.

Mr/Ms _____

Address _____

City/State _____ Zip _____

SK26-11/89

Please allow four to six weeks for delivery.
Prices and availability subject to change without notice.